THE ROYAL BALLET SCHOOL

Diaries

8

Second Year

Boys or
Ballet?

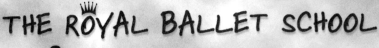

THE ROYAL BALLET SCHOOL

Diaries

8

Second Year

Boys or Ballet?

Written by Alexandra Moss

Grosset & Dunlap

Special thanks to Sue Mongredien

For the real Alice Granlund, with lots of love—A.M.

GROSSET & DUNLAP
Published by the Penguin Group
Penguin Group (USA) Inc., 375 Hudson Street, New York, New York 10014, U.S.A.
Penguin Group (Canada), 90 Eglinton Avenue East, Suite 700, Toronto, Ontario, Canada M4P 2Y3
(a division of Pearson Penguin Canada Inc.)
Penguin Books Ltd, 80 Strand, London WC2R 0RL, England
Penguin Ireland, 25 St Stephen's Green, Dublin 2, Ireland
(a division of Penguin Books Ltd)
Penguin Group (Australia), 250 Camberwell Road, Camberwell, Victoria 3124, Australia
(a division of Pearson Australia Group Pty Ltd)
Penguin Books India Pvt Ltd, 11 Community Centre, Panchsheel Park, New Delhi - 110 017, India
Penguin Group (NZ), Cnr Airborne and Rosedale Roads, Albany, Auckland 1310, New Zealand
(a division of Pearson New Zealand Ltd)
Penguin Books (South Africa) (Pty) Ltd, 24 Sturdee Avenue, Rosebank, Johannesburg 2196, South Africa

Penguin Books Ltd, Registered Offices:
80 Strand, London WC2R 0RL, England

Series created by Working Partners Ltd.

Copyright © 2006 by Working Partners Ltd. All rights reserved. Published by Grosset & Dunlap,
a division of Penguin Young Readers Group, 345 Hudson Street, New York, New York 10014.
GROSSET & DUNLAP is a trademark of Penguin Group (USA) Inc. Printed in the U.S.A.

Library of Congress Control Number: 2006007605

ISBN 0-448-44251-5   10 9 8 7 6 5 4 3 2 1

Prologue

Dear Diary,

Back to school again tomorrow—hooray! I'm always excited about going back to The Royal Ballet School, of course, but this time I'm counting down the minutes!

I still have to pinch myself to make sure that I'm not imagining things when I think back to that moment when I KISSED LUKE BAILEY the day before we left for half-term vacation and he asked me to be his girl-friend! I've had to live through eight whole days without seeing him since then, and it's seemed like the longest eight days of my whole life! I just can't WAIT to see him again tomorrow.

It feels really weird to think that I, Ellie Brown, have a boyfriend. My first boyfriend . . . it makes me feel all fluttery and fizzy inside. I'm kind of nervous as well, though. What are the rules? What do girlfriends DO? What's going to happen? I can't really imagine what it'll be like having a boyfriend at The Royal Ballet School. I know it won't be like regular dating I've read about in magazines, where your boyfriend comes to pick you up at your house to go on dates—I mean, that can't really happen at school, can it?

When I told the other girls at the end of last term they began teasing me (but in a nice way) saying, "Ooh, Ellie and Luke!" and giggling and pretending to kiss their pillows. Then, of course, they wanted to know ALL the details. How long had I liked him? What was it like to kiss a boy? All that stuff. It was good to be able to talk to them about it openly after covering up my feelings for so long beforehand. But there's one thing I'm kind of worried about: What if Luke stops liking me—or we argue? We'll still have to see each other every day—in class, as well as out of it! I guess Luke and I will just have to make things up as we go along . . .

There's a whole heap of other stuff to look forward to as well, though: Auditions will start soon for The Royal Ballet's Christmas production at The Royal Opera

House—and this year it's Swan Lake! I soooo hope I'm going to get a part. Dancing in The Nutcracker last Christmas was one of the most exciting, amazing, overwhelming things ever. And I can't wait to see Grace, Lara, and the other girls, too, of course!

Chapter 1

As her mom parked the car in The Royal Ballet Lower School driveway, Ellie Brown unclipped her seatbelt and wrenched open the car door.

"Be careful!" said her mom, sounding amused. "We might need that door again someday, Ellie."

Ellie blushed. "Sorry, Mom," she replied. "I'm just so excited!"

Mrs. Brown smiled. "I kind of guessed that," she said.

Ellie's cell phone began to ring and she rummaged through her bag to find it. Luke's number was on the screen. "Hello?" she said breathlessly.

"Hi, Ellie," came Luke's friendly voice. He sounded as if he was smiling. "Where are you? Are you nearly at school?"

Ellie found herself grinning. "I just arrived. Where are you?"

"I'm in the reception area," Luke told her. "I got here about half an hour ago. Shall I wait here for you?"

"Yes," Ellie said. Her heart raced at the thought of seeing him again. "I'll be right there."

She clicked her phone off and beamed at her mom, who'd heaved Ellie's two bags out of the trunk of the car.

"So . . . am I about the meet the mysterious Luke Bailey?" her mom asked with a smile.

Ellie felt herself blushing. She couldn't decide if she felt more excited—or nervous—or shy—or plain old embarrassed at the thought of introducing Luke and her mom to each other. "Um . . . I guess," she said slowly. "But only if you promise not to say anything awful about me, though—like any embarrassing things about when I was a baby, or dumb things I might have done, or . . ."

Her mom put Ellie's bags down and put an arm around her. "Hey," she said with a smile, "don't worry, I'll just say hello, that's all. Okay? Am I allowed to do that?"

Ellie nodded. "Okay," she said, and then bent down to peer in the side view mirror of the car. "Do I look all right?" she fretted. "Oh, I *knew* I should have blow-dried my hair more carefully this morning! It's all flyaway and wispy, and . . ."

Her mom gave her shoulder a reassuring squeeze. "Ellie, your hair is fine—you look lovely. You always look lovely," she said calmly.

Ellie took a deep breath and hoisted one of her bags up onto her shoulder. "Thanks, Mom," she said with a nervous smile. "Let's go, then."

They walked the short distance up to the entrance of White Lodge, the magnificent Georgian building that housed The Royal

Ballet Lower School.

Knowing that Luke might be watching her as she walked toward school made Ellie feel conscious of everything her body was doing. *Do I always walk so stiffly?* she wondered to herself. *Luke's going to think he has a robot for a girlfriend!* She smothered a hysterical giggle and, somehow or other, managed to get herself to the front doors, which were both opened wide. She held her breath as she went in . . . and there he was. Luke Bailey, his thumbs tucked into his jeans pockets, smiling broadly at her.

Ellie felt herself flush crimson as she smiled back. Not only had she lost control of her arms and legs, she seemed to have no say whatsoever in the colors her face turned today!

"Hi, Ellie," Luke said, stepping closer.

"Hi, Luke," she replied breathlessly. It felt very hot in the reception—or was that just her? She smiled again, feeling awkward. "Um . . . Luke? This is my mom. Mom, this is Luke. Luke Bailey."

Ellie's mom stepped forward with a friendly expression on her face. "Pleased to meet you, Luke," she said.

Now it was Luke's turn to look a little awkward. He gave her mom a polite smile, the kind of smile he'd give a teacher. "Hi, Mrs. Brown," he said.

There was a brief silence, and then Ellie asked, "Have your parents already gone, Luke?" She tried to sound conversational, but really she was wondering if she would have to go through the awkwardness of meeting *them*. She hoped not! She didn't really feel ready for that yet—not when she and Luke were still getting to know one another.

He nodded. "I waved them off about five minutes ago. Then I called you"—he held up his phone a little self-consciously—"and here you are!"

"Here I am," Ellie echoed, blushing all over again.

"Should we take these bags to your dorm, Ellie?" her mom prompted.

Ellie hesitated. It'd been a whole week since she'd seen Luke, and now she was going to have to leave him again! But she couldn't exactly expect her mom to hang around in the reception area while the two of them caught up. "Okay," she replied. "Um . . ."

"I'll meet you in half an hour or so, shall I?" Luke said. "Maybe on the Salon balcony?"

Ellie nodded. "Great," she said, beaming at him. "See you then!"

•   •   •   •

The dormitory setup for the Year 8 girls was slightly different from the year before. There was one large room, the Billiard Room, which was divided by an extended wall into two sides, known as the West End and the East End. There was also a smaller room, known as the Room Off, which led to the Billiard Room. That was where Ellie, Grace, Bryony, and Molly all slept.

Up in her dorm, Ellie saw that she was the first to arrive. She dumped her bags at the foot of her bed, then rushed over to the window. From there, you could just about see the old stone balcony outside the Salon, with its pink speckled steps that led down to the school grounds. The low, wintry sun was catching the tops of the trees, lighting up the last golden leaves that still clung to the branches. Ellie's heart jumped in her chest as she saw Luke step out of the Salon door onto the balcony. He was there already!

She backed away quickly from the window in case he turned and caught her watching him.

"Everything all right?" her mom asked curiously, coming over to see what Ellie was looking at.

"Mom! Don't look out the window! Luke's down there!" Ellie cried urgently. The thought of Luke seeing her mom spying out the window—even if she wasn't really *spying*—was even worse!

Mrs. Brown laughed. "All right, all right!" she said, holding her hands up. "I can see you'd much rather be there than here," she said, "so I'll just say good-bye now."

Ellie felt awful then. She didn't want her mom to feel unwelcome, or in the way at all! "Oh, Mom, I didn't mean—" she blurted out.

Her mom pulled her in for a hug. "He seems very nice," she whispered, and Ellie felt herself relax again.

"He *is* nice," Ellie agreed, hugging her mom back.

"I guess I'll be going, then," her mom said, kissing the top of

Ellie's head. "You don't have to walk me down to the car. Go and meet your Luke."

"Thanks for understanding, Mom," Ellie said as she walked her mom to the door and hugged her.

Ellie raced back to the window and peeped out of it cautiously. Luke was still there, leaning on the balcony, wrapping his arms around himself for warmth.

Ellie felt a pulse of excitement throb inside her. She ran to the bathroom and stared at herself in one of the mirrors. "Hi, Luke," she said in a casual voice, arching one eyebrow. She giggled. *No, not like that, I don't want to frighten him off,* she thought. "Hi, Luke," she tried again, trying to smile as prettily as she could.

She splashed some water on her cheeks, trying to cool them down, and then smiled for real at her reflection. "Hello," she said softly, staring intently at all of her features. Had Luke noticed that little scar in her eyebrow? What did he make of her turned up nose—the light scattering of freckles on it? Did he like her hair up in a ponytail, or down around her shoulders? Had he noticed that one of her ears was ever so slightly higher up than the other?

She stepped back from the mirror and smoothed out the pink fleece she was wearing. "Go on, then," she told her reflection. "Before poor Luke freezes out there!"

She hummed as she clattered down the stairs and into the reception area, which was full of students arriving, along with their parents. Ellie wove her way through them and into the Salon—once a large, formal reception room and now used as a ballet studio.

Luke was still leaning against the balcony, looking out over the grounds. He hadn't heard her arrive. Ellie stopped and just drank in the sight of him for a few moments. He looked so tall and rangy. And she sooo loved the way his hair was cropped close at the back of his neck, like soft moleskin. Her fingers itched to touch it.

Taking a deep breath, she stepped forward again and walked out onto the balcony. "Hi, Luke," she said. Her voice sounded strange, extra-loud.

He turned around. "Hi again," he said, his blue, blue eyes lighting up as he saw her. "That was quick!" he added.

Ellie felt her face flood with color again. Oh, no! Did she seem too keen? Should she have hung around a while longer in the dorm, and made him wait? She wrapped her arms around herself. It really was chilly outside, and all of a sudden she felt self-conscious.

Luke reached out and took one of her hands in his, his eyes soft. "I'm glad," he said.

Ellie's fingers tingled against the warmth of Luke's. Suddenly she wasn't sure what to say. They'd had no problem keeping up a conversation on the phone, or with text messages and emails for the whole of the half-term vacation, and yet now they were actually here again, face to face . . . where should she start? She seemed to have forgotten about half her vocabulary.

"So . . . um . . . how was your trip back here?" she began, and then covered her face with her free hand. "Sorry—what a boring question. Forget I asked that! Let me just think of something else to say . . ."

"Whoa, Ellie," Luke laughed. "It's all right—it wasn't a boring question. We had a really *eventful* journey, actually. My dad drove most of the way—and got stopped by the police for speeding on the motorway. So then my mum told him off, and took over the driving, only she's the slowest, most careful driver in the world! And then we had to stop because my little brother thought he was going to be sick . . ."

"Lovely," Ellie commented, with a grin. "And you still managed to get here before me!" she said.

Luke laughed. "Anyway, that's enough about my mad family. I'm just glad they went off before you had to meet them."

"Me too," Ellie confessed, and then put her hand up to her mouth. "Sorry—that sounds really rude! I don't mean it in a horrible way . . ."

Ellie was relieved to see that Luke was grinning. "I know, it's a bit weird, isn't it, the whole meeting-parents thing?" he said. "Your mum must think I'm a right idiot. I barely said a word to her."

"No! She thought you were nice!" Ellie assured him. "You did fine, I—" Hearing a tapping sound she stopped and looked around, but saw nothing.

"Up there," Luke said, pointing towards her dorm window. "It's the welcoming committee."

Ellie looked up to see Grace and Bryony knocking on the dorm window and waving at them.

Bryony opened the window. "Hi Ellie, hi Luke—we thought at first that it was Romeo and Juliet down there on the balcony!" she called teasingly. "It's teatime in a minute, by the way!"

"Okay, thanks!" Ellie called back. As Bryony shut the dorm window, Ellie turned to Luke and made a face. "Romeo and Juliet? Give us a break!" she said.

But Luke was laughing, his hand still around Ellie's. "It's getting a bit nippy out here, Juliet, don't you think?" he asked. "Would you care to accompany me to the banqueting room?"

Ellie giggled. "You mean, the canteen?" she said. "Sure thing, Romeo!"

•   •   •   •

In the canteen, Ellie saw that most of her Year 8 friends seemed to be back by now. There was Lara, with her distinctive red ponytail, and there was Molly laughing about something or other, and there was Grace, too, rushing over to join her and Luke.

"Hi, guys," Grace said warmly, hugging Ellie and collecting a tray from the stack. "I thought when I first arrived that the body-snatchers must have taken you away, Ell—I saw all your stuff dumped by the bed but no person! Did you just rush straight in and out?"

"Something like that," Ellie said, sharing a secret smile with

Luke. "How are you, anyway? Did you have a good week?"

"Really good," Grace replied, helping herself to a baked potato. "Totally stress-free, lots of Mum-and-me time, and lots of dog-walking!"

Ellie grinned, happy to see her friend looking so relaxed these days—a far cry from the uptight, tense Grace of last year.

After they'd served themselves, the three of them went to sit down with the rest of the Year 8 students at one of the long canteen tables. As Ellie tucked into her food and joined in the lively chatter, she was constantly aware of Luke's presence beside her and had to stop herself from beaming idiotically the whole time. Life at The Royal Ballet School was already amazing—but it felt even more special with a boyfriend to share it!

•　　　•　　　•　　　•

After tea, Ellie persuaded Grace, Molly, and Lara to play pool with the boys. Luke was there, of course, and Matt, who was a good friend of Ellie's, plus Danny and Nick.

There were too many of them to play doubles, so Ellie, Luke, and Molly volunteered to sit out for the first game.

"So first up could be Grace and Lara against Danny and Nick," suggested Molly. "Then Ellie and Luke, you can take on me and Matt. What do you think?"

Matt winked at Ellie. "I think we'll have an easy match, Molls," he said. "Those two lovebirds will be so busy gazing into each other's eyes, they won't pocket a single ball!"

Luke laughed. "Ahh—that's what you think, Matty-boy," he replied easily. "Haven't you heard of the lovebird bluff? It's a classic pool-player's strategy!"

"Fool the opposition—then wipe the floor with them," Ellie added, giggling. She loved sitting there with Luke's fingers around hers. It felt like the nicest thing in the world.

Matt rolled his eyes and grinned. "You can talk the talk, but can you walk the walk?" he asked. "I don't think so."

The first game of pool ended quickly, and then it was Ellie and Luke's turn to play Matt and Molly. Ellie felt as if she was walking through a dream. Whenever she leaned low over the pool table to take a shot, she would find her attention drifting to how nice it had been, holding hands with Luke—and she'd promptly hit the wrong ball.

"What did I say, Molls?" Matt said in a loud stage whisper. "She's gone to pieces!"

"I don't care," Ellie said happily, hitting the white ball by mistake.

"We'd noticed!" Molly laughed. "Oops!"

All too soon, it was time for the students to get ready for bed. One by one, the others drifted away until there was just Ellie and Luke left by the pool table.

"I had a really nice time tonight," Luke said, smiling at Ellie. He put one hand up to her cheek and held it lightly.

"Me too," Ellie said, feeling giddy. "It was fun."

Luke leaned forward and kissed Ellie, a sweet, gentle kiss that left her legs feeling trembly. "Good night, Ellie," he said. "I think I'm going to enjoy this term."

Ellie felt as if she could hardly get a word out, she was so dizzy from Luke's kiss. "Me too," she said at last.

Dear Diary,

I've had such a great day. I'm back at school and I'm back with Luke, my boyfriend. (I still get a kick out of writing that!) We hung out together all evening playing pool with Matt and a couple of the other kids. Some of the other girls were watching a movie on TV, but I really wanted to be with Luke.

I like him soooo much!

Better go—I still haven't unpacked properly yet and Mrs. Parrish is due to come round any moment for lights out!

Chapter 2

On Monday mornings, Ellie had English, chemistry, and drama lessons. She always sat next to Grace for all of her academic lessons—but was thrilled when Luke came over with Matt to take the two desks next to them in their first lesson. Ellie beamed across at Luke as he sat down.

"This morning we're going to start a new Shakespeare play," Ms. Swaisland, their English teacher, said. "It's one I'm sure most of you will already know something of: *Romeo and Juliet.*"

Grace elbowed Ellie's side and gave her a knowing grin.

Ellie rolled her eyes in reply. She wasn't sure she liked the sound of this!

"Would anyone like to tell the class what they know of the story?" Ms. Swaisland invited.

"I think Ellie might, Miss," Grace said mischievously.

Ms. Swaisland turned her gaze upon Ellie. "Ellie, would you like to?" she asked, with an expectant smile.

Ellie glanced quickly at Luke who winked back. She cleared her throat. "Um . . ." she started, racking her brains. "Well, I

only know the ballet, really. I haven't read the play," she said
apologetically. "Romeo and Juliet are in love, but their families
don't get along so they have to sneak around behind their parents'
backs. Then they get caught—and it all goes wrong, and . . . um . . .
well, they die in the end, don't they?" she finished, feeling rather
flustered.

"Thank you, Ellie—that's a good start," Ms. Swaisland said.
"Does anybody know anything else about this play?"

As Lara put her hand up and began to speak, Ellie turned to
Grace. "Grace, you really put me on the spot!" she whispered.

"Sorry—I couldn't resist," Grace replied cheekily.

Ellie looked across at Luke who shrugged. "You know
more than I do about it, if that makes you feel any better," he
whispered.

It did, a little. Ellie felt as if he was on her side, which was the
main thing. "So you're not going to dump me because I'm not a
Shakespeare scholar?" she giggled.

Luke pretended to consider the question. "We-e-ell . . ." he
said playfully.

". . . and do you think they were right to do so, Luke?" Ms.
Swaisland's voice suddenly cut into their conversation.

Now it was Luke's turn to be on the spot. He scratched his
head uncertainly. "Oh, yes, definitely . . ." he guessed.

Ms. Swaisland raised her eyebrows. "Really?" she asked,
sounding surprised. "You think Romeo and Juliet's parents were
right to forbid the young lovers from seeing one another?"

Luke shifted uncomfortably on his chair. "Oh, no! Sorry, Miss . . . I wasn't paying attention," he confessed. "I think the parents were *wrong*."

Ms. Swaisland nodded. "Me too. So do I have everybody's attention now? Good. Then let's start reading the play itself." She handed out copies of the text to each student. "Any volunteers to be our romantic leads?" she said.

Ellie kept her hand firmly down. She didn't want to draw any more attention to herself in a Juliet role, thank you very much— and besides, Luke had just slipped her a note that she wanted to read instead.

Hope our families don't decide to argue over us, like R+J's did over them! he'd written.

Ellie grinned. *You're safe—my mom said she liked you, remember?* she wrote back.

The paper came back moments later. *Ah, but she hasn't met my lunatic parents yet, has she? They're sure to turn her against all members of the Bailey clan in a second!*

Ellie giggled out loud, and tried to turn it into a cough. Luckily, Ms. Swaisland had just asked everybody to turn to the first page of the play, so her giggle was drowned out by the sound of rustling paper.

"What's so funny?" Grace wanted to know, smoothing down the page in her book.

Ellie showed her the note. "Luke says my mom will think his parents are crazy," she said.

Grace drew a smiley face on the note. *Grace says hi,* Ellie wrote. *Don't worry—all parents sometimes act like lunatics.*

"Is that a note being passed around at the back there?" Ms. Swaisland said sharply, just as Ellie had pushed it onto Luke's desk.

Luke covered it with his arm. "No, Miss," he said, his eyes wide.

Ms. Swaisland frowned at him. "I hope not," she said. "Because the only thing you should be reading is this play." There was a moment's silence, and then Ms. Swaisland went on. "Right—Act One, Scene One—let's begin . . ."

The lesson passed by quickly. Ellie found it very hard to concentrate with Luke sitting there. She tried—she really tried!— to focus on what was being read aloud, but it was difficult to tune in to the Shakespearean language when all she could think about was Luke sitting so close to her.

During the more romantic passages of the play, she found herself looking at Luke and smiling. She knew exactly how Juliet must have felt!

Unfortunately, a little later, she was so busy doodling love hearts all over the back of her English notebook that she missed what Ms. Swaisland was saying about English prep. "What was the assignment?" she asked Grace with a jump, as the rest of the class started piling up their books and getting to their feet.

Grace chuckled. "Ellie Brown, you really were in your own little world just then, weren't you?" she said, her English books already back in her bag. "I'll show you later," she added. She walked toward the classroom door. "Come on, let's catch up with Lara."

As she followed Grace, Ellie looked around for Luke and saw that he was right behind her. When he caught up to her in the corridor, he took her hand. Somebody whistled behind them— Matt, it sounded like—and Ellie felt the tips of her ears turn red.

"Hey, maybe we could be lab partners in chemistry today?" Luke suggested.

Ellie looked ahead to where Grace was chatting animatedly with Lara and Isabelle. "Well . . . I usually pair up with Grace," she faltered, feeling torn. Part of her wanted to agree instantly to Luke's idea, but she'd been friends with Grace for a long time and the last thing she wanted to do was snub her.

Luke smiled, not taking offense at being turned down. "That's okay," he said, and then laughed. "Actually, maybe being partners in class is not such a good idea, if that English lesson was anything to go by. I just couldn't get into it today. I kept really trying to listen to what Ms. Swaisland was saying, but all I could think about was . . ." He cast a sidelong glance at Ellie. ". . . was how pretty you look today," he said, dropping his eyes suddenly.

"Oh, thank you . . ." Ellie replied, feeling shy and thrilled all at the same time. There was a moment's silence, so she quickly tried to lighten it. "You charmer, you!" she added with a grin.

Luke laughed. "That's me," he agreed. "And come to think of it, being partners in chemistry is *definitely* a bad idea. I'd probably blow up the school or something, because I'd be too busy looking at you rather than listening to what the teacher was telling us!"

Ellie chuckled but couldn't help brushing a protective hand along the corridor wall. "Don't even *joke* about blowing up this place, Luke Bailey," she told him. "That is sooo not funny!"

•   •   •   •

After chemistry and drama came lunch, and then it was time for ballet class. Ellie felt a shiver of happiness as she peeled off her sweatpants in the studio and made her way across to the barre to start warming up. Ballet *and* Luke—what a combination. She was going to have a permanent grin on her face now that she had *two* such wonderful things in her life!

Ms. Black, the Year 8 ballet teacher, came into the studio a few minutes later. "Welcome back to school, everybody," she said, smiling around at them all. "I hope everyone has had a good half-term break."

Isabelle Armand immediately put a hand up. "Ms. Black, do you know when the auditions for *Swan Lake* are?" she wanted to know.

Ellie looked over at her friend's expectant face. Isabelle had missed out on the chance to audition for last year's Royal Ballet Christmas production of *The Nutcracker*—and she was clearly desperate for a chance to audition this year.

"I do know, yes," Ms. Black replied. "Auditions for *Swan Lake* start this Friday."

An excited gasp went around the studio, and Ms. Black smiled and went on. "Auditions will be observed classes," she said, "as they were last year. So you won't have any particular preparation to do—you will just turn up to class as usual and have a regular lesson. The only difference will be that The Royal Ballet Director and her colleagues will be sitting in, watching the whole thing." She grinned. "You'll barely notice them!"

"Oh, sure!" Lara laughed.

"I know it feels strange, having them observing you," Ms. Black sympathized, "but I've been told they'll be here for the full lesson, so hopefully by the end of that time, you'll have gotten over the trauma of being watched in an audition situation and will all produce some excellent ballet."

She consulted a piece of paper in her hand. "There will, as usual, be two cast lists—Cast A and Cast B. And in this ballet, roles for Lower School students are all for girls. The parts up for grabs are the little swans in Act Two—and there are also roles for two girls in Act One." Ellie found that she was gripping the barre extra tightly with excitement. She so wanted to be chosen!

"Right, then . . ." Ms. Black concluded, "we'd better get started. Because if anybody's feeling rusty after the half-term break, we need to knock those rust spots off before Friday!"

•　　•　　•　　•

That evening Ellie and her friends discussed the Christmas production as they got changed for supper.

"Early nights this week, girls," Grace said, brushing out her hair. "We've all got to be in top form on Friday!"

"I am so excited," Molly confessed, wriggling into her jeans, "even though I know I won't get picked!"

"Why not?" Ellie asked. "Okay, you've only been at The Royal Ballet School for half a term—but you're a great dancer!"

Molly smiled ruefully. "But we all know I've still got some catching up to do," she replied. "Don't worry, Ellie, you don't have to try and cheer me up. I'm not feeling sorry for myself or fishing for compliments. I'm just stating facts." She plucked a top out of her wardrobe and slid it off its hanger. "It's cool. Just auditioning will be exciting enough—for this year, anyway!" she added with a grin.

Grace grimaced. "You've got a great attitude, Molly," she said. "You're so calm about it all, chances are you won't get flustered in the audition and fall to pieces—like I usually do."

Ellie shot Grace a sympathetic look. She'd seen Grace crumble under pressure several times now, and it was awful to watch. "Well *I* think we've *all* got a good chance," she said staunchly. "Let's aim for four out of four of us Room Off girls!"

Dear Diary,

The first day back has been great! It was really exciting hearing more about the Swan Lake auditions. I'm going to practice hard all week to prepare for Friday. So much for Grace's plan for early nights, though . . . I spent all evening playing pool with Luke and some of the others again. I was on a bit of a roll tonight—I was sinking balls every time I took the cue. I love it when that happens.

The Year 8 boys are all disappointed that there are no boys' roles in this year's Royal Ballet Christmas production. I think Luke was especially put out; he just missed out on a role in The Nutcracker last year. He said he'd practice with me tomorrow evening, though—I think Grace and Matt are going to join us, too. Dancing with Luke . . . oh, it's just going to be heavenly!!

"If you could all turn to your prep first, please, we'll go through it together," said Ms. Swaisland.

Ellie felt a sick feeling spread through her chest as she took in the English teacher's words. Around her, the whole class was opening their exercise books. The whole class except for her, that was. Ellie had never even gotten around to copying the assignment details from Grace, let alone doing the actual work. Her head had been so full of Luke, she'd forgotten all about it!

Ellie sighed down at the line of love-hearts she'd doodled during the last lesson, and then turned to Grace. "Grace . . . can I look at yours, please?" she hissed. "Sorry, I never managed to . . ."

Grace pushed over her exercise book so that it was spread out between the two of them.

"Paraphrasing exercise, Act One, Scene One," Ellie read in Grace's neat handwriting. She felt even sicker as she saw how much work Grace had done, translating two or three pages of the Shakespeare into modern English. Yet Grace had been dancing in the studio along with Ellie, Luke, and Matt the night before. "When did you do all this?" she whispered to Grace.

"Monday night," Grace whispered back.

Ahh. When Ellie had been playing pool with Luke. "I can't believe I forgot to do this," she whispered again. "You're a lifesaver, Grace."

"Paramedic Grace, that's me," Grace replied. But her smile didn't quite reach her eyes, Ellie noticed. Oh no. Was Grace mad at her?

"So, is everyone ready?" Ms. Swaisland went on. She looked at Oliver Stafford and Simon Down, who were sitting right at the front. "Gentlemen, if you'd be so kind as to begin, please? Oliver, would you read out your paraphrasing of Montague's two questions—and Simon, give us your version of Benvolio's answers."

Ellie felt really uncomfortable as she sat listening. She'd never forgotten to do prep like this, never. Even when they'd had exams and rehearsals for the summer show at the end of last term, she'd still managed to stay on top of everything.

Business before pleasure, Ellie! That was what her mom always said whenever she'd make herself pay a pile of bills or do some ironing or sort out the washing, when really all she wanted to do was watch TV or read a book. Ellie had heard that saying so many times when she was growing up. But she'd gone and forgotten it, hadn't she, putting the pleasure of hanging out with Luke way in front of the business of her prep!

She flicked her eyes across to Luke who seemed to have gotten *his* prep done okay. It was just her then, Head-in-the-Clouds Brown, who'd managed to forget.

The uneasy feeling stayed with Ellie for the whole lesson and at the end, when Ms. Swaisland asked them to leave their exercise books on her desk so that she could mark them, Ellie waited until everybody else had handed in theirs, then went up to her teacher.

"Ms. Swaisland? I'm really sorry, I forgot to do my prep," she confessed. "Is it all right if I hand it in tomorrow instead?"

Ms. Swaisland looked a little surprised at the request but nodded. "If you leave it in my pigeonhole first thing in the morning, we'll say no more about it," she said. "Please don't let this become a habit, though, Ellie. You've always been one of my hardest working pupils. I'd hate for that to change."

"I'd hate that, too, Ms. Swaisland," Ellie said, swallowing hard. She was feeling *really* guilty now! "You'll definitely have it first thing tomorrow. I'll deliver it before I've even had my breakfast!"

Ms. Swaisland smiled at that and shook her head. "So long as it's there before nine o'clock, that's fine," she said. "Don't starve yourself on account of Romeo and Juliet, Ellie!"

Ellie smiled back, and headed off to her next lesson. She was glad Ms. Swaisland hadn't come down too hard on her—but all the same, she didn't want to have to make another such confession. "From now on, it's definitely business before pleasure all the way," she reminded herself as she ran along the corridor towards the canteen for lunch.

"Do you always talk to yourself, Ellie, or only on Wednesdays?" came a familiar voice.

Ellie looked up and grinned as she saw Luke waiting for her at the end of the corridor. "Only when I've forgotten to do my prep," she replied. "I can't believe I just clean forgot like that!"

Luke slipped an arm through hers as they went to the canteen together. "Whatever could you have been thinking of?" he asked, teasingly.

"I think I'm walking along with him right now," Ellie replied, smiling up at him. Her heart bumped joyfully as she did so. Oh, he was so lovely!

Grace and the others were already in line at the canteen. "What did she say?" Grace asked, as Ellie and Luke picked up trays and joined the queue for food.

"Who?" Ellie asked.

"Ms. Swaisland!" said Grace. "What did she say about your prep?"

"Oh! She was all right," Ellie said sheepishly. Somehow being with Luke had made her forget all about the prep disaster. "I've got to do it tonight instead."

Luke looked a bit crestfallen. "I thought we were going to do some ballet together tonight," he said.

Ellie hesitated. She'd forgotten they'd agreed to meet up and dance again. "Well, maybe once I've done this prep," she said.

"It's a shame I've already handed mine in, otherwise you could have copied it," Luke said, ladling some vegetables onto his plate. "I'm sure it won't take you long, though—we might still get time for some ballet. What do you reckon?"

Ellie found herself weakening, but then Lara chipped in. "We've got that geography test tomorrow as well, remember," she said to the group.

Ellie sighed and spooned some potatoes onto her plate. "I guess I'll have to call a rain check on tonight, then," she told Luke. "Sorry."

Luke looked disappointed, but nodded. "Never mind," he replied, but the sparkle had left his eyes.

Ellie felt her resolve sway again. She put a hand on his arm. "But you know, I'm sure I'll have *some* time to hang out later," she said, trying to avoid Grace's eye. "After all, I do have a bit of a head start on the English prep now, after the paraphrasing in class this morning. I'll start on it during tuck and race through as much of it as I can. Then after supper, I'll come and do some ballet with you, and finish my English and do my geography stuff before bed. Deal?"

Luke smiled. "Deal."

•   •   •   •

Ellie stared at the first passage in her *Romeo and Juliet* text, trying hard to think back to her English lesson. How had Oliver translated the opening lines again? It all looked like a foreign language to her now. She'd been so thrown at having forgotten her prep she'd hardly been able to concentrate. And, after the tough ballet class she'd just had, she was starving, too! It was hard not to think about her friends having their tuck right now.

She put her pen down abruptly and got to her feet. She'd just run down, grab a bite to eat, and then come straight back up here . . .

Business before pleasure, a voice in her head reminded her at the door.

But eating IS business when you're a dancer, she argued with herself. *I'll be two minutes and then . . .*

Ellie saw the clock on the wall and her eyes widened in surprise. Two minutes was all she had left before she had to go to her next class, swimming. Oh, no! Her ballet class had run a little late today, and actually, there was no time to do anything else for her prep.

She grabbed her swimming stuff, then hurtled downstairs toward the canteen. She had to eat something before swimming—but she'd be doing it on the run!

•　　•　　•　　•

Ellie usually loved swimming. There was something calming about being surrounded by water; she loved the feeling of lightness as she moved through it, especially after a strenuous ballet class.

Today, however, she spent most of her swimming lesson

thinking about all the things she had to pack into the evening ahead. In addition to the English prep, there was the geography homework to grapple with, too. She hadn't so much as glanced at that yet. And then she was supposed to be meeting up with Luke . . .

And I've got to sleep at some point, she thought with a sigh. *When am I supposed to fit that in?*

•   •   •   •

"Coming to watch the movie?"

Ellie looked up to see Lara's head around the dorm door and shook her head regretfully. She was lying on her bed poring over her Shakespeare. "I've still got this English prep to do, and the geography revision as well," she replied. Over the half-term break, she'd forgotten all about the geography test Mr. Whitehouse had warned them about. Talk about a mean trick, giving a test in the first week back after half-term!

"How about you, Grace? Molly? Bryony?" Lara asked.

Grace, who had been diligently scribbling down her geography notes, sat up on her bed and stretched her arms above her head. "Yeah, count me in," she said. "It's one of my favorites. And I think I've just about got my geography straight in my head, too."

"Me too," Bryony said, getting to her feet. "Or as straight as it's going to be, anyway."

"I'll join you in a moment," Molly added. "I'm just writing my brother's birthday card."

Ellie heaved such a gusty sigh as Grace left the dorm that her page of *Romeo and Juliet* turned over. Her eye drifted to the top of the page:

ROMEO: Ay me! Sad hours seem long

"Couldn't have put it better myself, Romeo," Ellie muttered, flipping back to her place on the page before reading on.

MONTAGUE: Many a morning hath he there been seen,
With tears augmenting the fresh morning dew.

"Oh, help . . ." Ellie groaned. "This is going to take forever! What does 'augmenting' mean?"

"Adding," Molly called out, overhearing Ellie's mutterings. "Augmenting means adding. You must be at the bit where Montague's talking about Romeo's tears *adding* to the morning's dew," she said helpfully.

Ellie put her dictionary down. "How come you find it so easy?" she asked.

"Teamwork," Molly explained. "On Monday night, Grace, Bryony, and I worked it all out together. *Much* easier that way."

"Well, you can definitely count me in next time," Ellie said with a wry grin.

Molly went off to the common room to join the others and

watch the movie while Ellie plowed on until she'd finished the passages Ms. Swaisland had assigned. There. It was a bit rushed, to be honest, and she knew she could have done a better job with more time, but . . . well, she didn't have more time. Simple as that. She'd do the next prep assignment *properly,* she vowed. She'd spend ages on it. And then everything would feel right again.

It was eight o'clock and Ellie shot a guilty look at her geography books sitting on her bedside table, untouched, before she pulled on her ballet things to go and meet Luke. *Just half an hour of dancing, and then I'll be right back to study,* she promised herself, slipping quickly out of the dorm.

Her heart stepped up a beat as she reached the practice studio where Luke had said he'd be—only to see him in there with Matt and Alice. Luke was twirling Alice around and they were both giggling about something or other. Ellie felt an uncomfortable thud in her chest. What was going on? Luke had talked about wanting to dance with *her* tonight like it was a big deal to him. Yet here he was, goofing around with Alice!

Ellie bit her lip, trying not to feel jealous as she pushed the door open. "Hi, guys," she said, deliberately not catching Luke's eye as she put on her ballet shoes. *Keep your cool,* she told herself. She'd been convinced that Luke and Alice liked each other at the start of fall term, back in September, and had been sure that Luke wanted *Alice* to be his girlfriend. She'd gotten over that, sure—but one look at them tonight had brought the jealous feelings flooding back.

"Hey, Ellie—I was starting to think you weren't coming," Luke said, coming over and putting a hand on her back. "We thought we'd wait until you got here before we made a proper start. Alice came to join us. Okay?"

Ellie smiled, and her jealousy melted away. "Okay," she said. "Give me two minutes to warm up. What are we going to work on first?"

"Well, Matt and I both need to practice our *tours en l'air*," Luke said, "so maybe we could get started on those while you warm up."

"And I'm still not sure about those *sissonnes*," Alice added. "Even though Ms. Black made us do about five hundred of them this afternoon. Fancy going through a few with me, once you're ready?"

Ellie smiled. "Sure," she said. "I'll be right with you." She glanced up at the clock on the wall. "I've only got until eight thirty tonight, though—I've not even looked at my geography stuff yet. Have you guys?"

Luke shrugged. "Kind of. A little bit over the holidays. There's not much to review, though, Ellie. It's only stuff about Britain—major cities, import and export goods, industries, population spread, that kind of thing. A lot of it is general knowledge."

Ellie made a face. "General knowledge if you've lived in Britain all your life," she reminded him. Ellie and her mom had only been living in England for just over two years. She was still a bit hazy about where different cities were—and she certainly had no idea about imports and exports. "I, on the other hand, definitely need to bone up on this one!"

Ellie turned to the barre and tried to clear her mind of geography and schoolwork, instead focusing on what her body was doing. She thought about her muscles lengthening and stretching, about the position of her fingers, about the curve of her neck. Soon she was relaxing into the familiar warm-up routine that she'd done hundreds of times before.

She and Alice worked on their *sissonnes,* and then all four of them worked really hard on their *grands jetés.*

Ellie was enjoying the ballet so much that she was quite shocked when she looked up and saw that it was quarter to nine already. "Oh my gosh!" she gasped, running over to grab her sweat suit. "It's time to go, guys—lights out in fifteen minutes!"

"Hey—don't run off so fast!" Luke said, coming after her. "We haven't said good night yet." He held her in his arms and kissed her gently, then brushed a tendril of hair out of her eyes. "That was fun," he said, smiling.

Ellie smiled back. There was something about Luke's face that just made everything seem all right, somehow. "Any time," she said, suddenly feeling a little shy at the way he was looking at her. "But I've really got to fly. I'll have to study my geography by flashlight tonight."

Alice came over and pulled on her sweat suit, too. "Night, boys," she said. "See you in the morning!"

Ellie and Alice ran up to the dorm where Ellie just had time to jump in the shower, brush her teeth, and pull on her pajamas before their housemother, Mrs. Parrish, came around to turn the lights out and wish them all good night.

Ellie's heart was thumping as adrenaline coursed around her. She hadn't even *looked* at her geography stuff yet—and their lesson was first thing tomorrow morning! She was going to be in so much trouble if she completely flunked the test, which, let's face it, she was going to. There was only so much guesswork a girl could get away with.

"Are you all right, Ellie?" Grace asked, watching Ellie wriggling into her pajama top. "You seem a bit . . . stressed."

"That's because I am," Ellie replied grimly. "I'm so going to fail this test tomorrow. I lost track of time, and—"

"Good night, girls," came Mrs. Parrish's voice, and she appeared in the doorway. "Everybody ready for lights out?"

"Just about," Ellie said, hopping into bed quickly. Her hair was still wet and felt cold on her pillow. She hoped Mrs. Parrish wouldn't notice.

"Good night, then," Mrs. Parrish said, and switched the lights off. "See you in the morning."

"Good night," the girls chorused.

As soon as Mrs. Parrish had left the dorm, Ellie flicked on her flashlight and sat up with her geography book. She felt really tired after working—and dancing—so hard all day, but she had no choice. She had to memorize at least *some* facts about Britain—otherwise she'd really pay for it in the morning!

• • • •

"Good morning, girls! Shake a leg!"

Ellie groaned at the sound of Mrs. Parrish's voice. Was it really morning already? She'd had awful dreams about being in a touring company and missing the tour bus. She had to find all the cities on her own—London, Birmingham, Manchester, Edinburgh, the capital of Wales—but she couldn't because she hadn't been able to memorize them.

"Are you all right, Ellie?" Molly asked sympathetically as Ellie lay in bed longer than usual. It was so hard, the thought of crawling out from under her duvet.

Ellie yawned. "Just tired," she said. "I didn't sleep very well. I kept thinking about the test this morning."

"It'll be fine," Bryony said reassuringly. "Mr. Whitehouse wouldn't give us a real toughie in the first week after half-term, would he?"

"Let's hope not," Ellie said, pushing off her duvet. "Ooh, let's hope he's forgotten all about it. Let's hope he suffered amnesia over the vacation and thinks he gave us the test last term. Or . . ."

"I think you must be still asleep, Ellie Brown," Grace said, shooting her a funny little smile. "You're certainly dreaming, anyway. Come on—it'll all be over by ten o'clock. Only three hours to go!"

Ellie felt as if she was sleepwalking through breakfast, but she managed a ten-minute cramming session before the nine o'clock geography class.

And then, just as she was about to walk into the classroom, she remembered she was supposed to be handing in her English prep to Ms. Swaisland! And her English notebook was sitting on her bedside table. "Oh, help—where's Romeo when you need him?" she muttered.

Luke raised a quizzical eyebrow, and she hurriedly explained.

"Sorry, not sure where old Romeo is just now," he said with a grin, "but I'll go and get your prep instead, if you like," he offered.

Ellie laughed. "No chance—you'd be in big trouble if anyone caught you," she reminded him. Boys and girls were not allowed in each other's dorms at any time.

"Are you sure?" Luke asked teasingly. "I could sneak a peek at that diary of yours while I was there . . ."

"I'm going, I'm going!" Ellie cried. "You can stop that thought right there, Luke Bailey!" There was absolutely no way she wanted Luke—or anybody else—to see her diary. Just the thought of it was enough to send her off at a record-breaking sprint.

Up in the dorm, she grabbed her English book, hurried down to thrust it into Ms. Swaisland's pigeonhole outside the staff room, and then rushed back to the geography room.

She burst in, red-faced, apologies spilling out of her. "Sorry, sir," she panted. "I had something to hand in—really urgent—sorry!"

Mr. Whitehouse smiled at her and put a finger to his lips. It was only then that Ellie realized the room was in complete silence. She looked around and saw that the rest of the class was already hard at work on the test.

"Sit down, Ellie," Mr. Whitehouse said. "There's a test paper on your desk. You've missed the first five minutes, so you'd better get a move on."

Ellie sat down, feeling totally flustered. She was hot from running, and her hair was springing out of her ponytail all over the place. She felt like she was chasing her tail, trying to keep up with everything—and the term had only just begun!

Dear Diary,
    Not the best day today: I got 3 out of 20 for the geography test!
    I didn't get much sympathy from Grace—who just pointed out that I had been spending a lot of time with Luke these last few evenings. So I pointed out that she watched a movie last night, so what was the difference?
    And then she said the difference was that she wouldn't have watched the movie if she hadn't done all her geography first! And she was pretty snippy about it! Which isn't like her at all.

I can't help wondering if Grace is maybe a bit jealous because I've got a boyfriend and she doesn't . . .

"Calm down, Molly. Deep breath. Calm down!"

Ellie looked along the barre to where Molly was staring into the mirror and talking sternly to herself. "Are you all right there, Molls?" she asked. Ellie had never seen her quite so pale and anxious before.

Molly looked embarrassed. "Kind of," she said, then laughed nervously. "No, actually, I'm not. I feel in a right flap about this audition class!"

It was Friday afternoon and the day of the *Swan Lake* casting class for the Year 8 girls. They were in their regular ballet studio, but the atmosphere was anything but ordinary. Everyone seemed jittery, Ellie included. Her ballet performance over the next two hours would determine whether or not she would be dancing on The Royal Opera House stage with The Royal Ballet this Christmas. Talk about pressure!

"It's daft," Molly went on, trying to smile. "I mean, I know already that I won't get picked—like I was saying the other night. Yet I still feel antsy about it. I know some of you guys have danced at The Royal Opera House already, but for me . . . it's still the stuff of best-ever dreams. And to know that the possibility is going to be so tantalizingly close—within touching distance . . ."

Further along the barre, Isabelle was nodding. "I feel like you," she assured Molly. "Although I have danced at The Royal Opera House in the summer performances, it was for one day only. I wasn't here for the Christmas performances last year either, and, like you, I am longing to be a part of it this time." A frown appeared between her eyebrows. "We must all dance better than we've ever danced before, I think. We must show that we could be the most graceful little swans the director has ever seen!"

Lara smiled. "Come on, then, you swans," she said to the others, turning back to the barre. "Let's get our wings warmed up—ready to impress those directors!"

Ellie turned to the barre herself, feeling the adrenaline coursing through her as she stretched out her body in the usual warm-up exercises. She gritted her teeth nervously, feeling as if she was a car revving up for a race. She so wanted to be a part of *Swan Lake*. It was one of her favorite ever ballets. She just *had* to dance her best today. She had to be perfect!

On the other side of Ellie, Grace was keeping quiet as she worked through her warm-up exercises. Ellie knew better than to talk to Grace about the selection class—chances were, Grace was feeling knotted up inside with nerves and wanted to block the whole thing out, rather than agonize out loud. *Poor Grace*, Ellie thought with a sudden rush of sympathy. *It must be awful to get so stressed about auditioning.*

"Good afternoon, everyone," came Ms. Black's voice.

Ellie paused in her exercises to turn to the front of the studio. "Good afternoon, Ms. Black," she replied, along with the rest of the class. And then Ellie felt herself stiffen as a man and woman, both carrying clipboards, followed Ms. Black into the studio. The directors of The Royal Ballet. Ellie felt a shiver go all the way down her back. The selection class was about to begin!

"Hello, everyone," the man said, holding up a hand in greeting. "My name is Alex, and this is Joanna. We're going to be sitting in on your class today."

Joanna, who had a chic dark bob and wore an elegant gray pants suit, smiled around at the class. "Please just ignore us," she said breezily. "You'll dance much better if you can put us out of your minds and concentrate on yourselves."

"Easier said than done," Molly muttered, gnawing on a fingernail. "Oh, help! This is real, isn't it?"

"You'll be fine," Ellie whispered back. "Try and relax."

"Finish warming up, please, ladies," Ms. Black said briskly, "and then we can begin."

Ellie turned back to the barre at once. *Focus, Ellie,* she told herself. *This really matters. You've got to shine like a true ballerina!*

The class began. Usually, Ellie found it fairly easy to focus completely on her dancing in a situation like this. If anything else drifted into her mind, she'd just sweep it out of there. Yet today, she was struggling to find that total concentration. All she could think of was how much she couldn't wait to see Luke after class.

In the center, Ms. Black instructed them to do a series of *sissonnes,* jumping off from two feet, but landing on one. Ellie forced herself to pay attention as their teacher demonstrated, glad that she'd fitted in that extra practice with Alice a few nights before.

After the *sissonnes* came a sequence of pose turns from the corner. Ms. Black asked the girls to line up along one side of the studio and perform the sequence across the room, one by one.

As she waited in line, Ellie's thoughts drifted to Luke again. How perfect it would be if she *did* get a part in the ballet, and Luke came to watch her . . .

"And . . . Ellie! Off you go!"

Ms. Black's voice jolted into Ellie's reverie and, for a split-second, she couldn't remember what she was supposed to be doing. Help! Oh, yes—of course, the pirouette sequence. She set off across the studio, trying to dance the steps exactly as Ms. Black had instructed them, spinning lightly on her toes.

It was only when she reached the other side that her heart started to thud. That had nearly gone so wrong! Ellie leaned against the barre, breathing deeply. For the rest of the class, she just had to lock Luke out of her mind!

•　　•　　•　　•

"That was awful," said Molly as she collapsed onto her bed, red in the face.

Ellie nodded. The selection class had been a grueling two hours for all of them—and Ellie knew she hadn't danced her very best. She'd managed to block out all thoughts of Luke for the rest of the session, but still cursed herself for drifting off earlier on. She desperately hoped the directors hadn't seen. "At least it's over," she sighed.

"Grace did sooo well," added Bryony. "You really held it together there, Grace—I didn't see any trace of nerves whenever I caught sight of you."

"Thanks!" Grace replied, looking flushed and happy. "It felt okay. It was the first audition I've had in ages where I actually felt like I did myself justice."

"Yes, you really did," Molly agreed warmly. "I was looking out for you, too, after everything you told us last night, and I was really impressed. Really, Grace, I'm not just saying it. They'd be mad not to pick you."

Ellie felt a little lost. Everything Grace had told them last night? What was Molly talking about?

Grace buried her face in the towel she was holding, embarrassed by all the praise. "Oh, you guys . . . you're just saying it to make me feel better!" she said.

Bryony shook her head vigorously. "No way. I wouldn't do that," she said. "I think you've cracked it, Grace. You've cracked your audition technique!"

Grace laughed delightedly. "I hope you're right. I would sooo love to get a part in this year's show!" she said. Still grinning, she left the dorm to go to the bathroom.

Ellie turned to Bryony. "What was all that about?" she asked in a low voice. "Was Grace freaking out last night, or something?"

Bryony nodded. "She got a bit stressed about the audition, yeah," she replied. "Molls and I had to give her a pep talk."

"Oh, right," Ellie said, feeling a bit hurt. So Grace had been really nervous yet hadn't confided in Ellie. Why not?

Because I was busy with Luke again last night, she answered herself. *That's why.* She knew it wasn't really a big deal—after all, she herself confided in people other than Grace at times. But the fact that Grace hadn't come to her first still stung a little. It wasn't so long ago that Ellie had always been the one Grace had called upon to coach her through those stressful times. And now it seemed she'd been replaced.

•   •   •   •

Luke gave Ellie a hug as he saw her coming into the canteen for tuck. "How was it? Did you do okay?" he asked.

Ellie grimaced. "It wasn't great," she said, leaning against him. It felt so good, standing like that, with his arms around her. "I mean, *I* wasn't great," she corrected ruefully. "I kept thinking about you, when I should have been thinking about ballet."

Luke rubbed her back. "Well, hopefully you were dancing with a smile on your face, then," he said, squeezing her tightly for a second.

Ellie felt herself smiling at his comforting words. "That's true," she said, feeling a little better. "Thanks, Luke. You always manage to cheer me up!"

•   •   •   •

"Hey, guys, the cast lists are going up after breakfast—I just heard one of the Year 9 girls say so!" Lara's face was alight with excitement as she made her announcement. It was Monday morning, and the Year 8 girls were lining up in the canteen.

"Oh wow, that was quick!" Ellie gulped. She hadn't been expecting to hear until much later in the week. She wasn't so sure she was ready to see the cast list. Ever since the selection class, she'd been growing more and more convinced that her poor concentration would have ruled her out for a part.

"Suddenly I've gone right off the idea of food," Grace wailed. "I feel sick! I just know I'm going to look at that list and see everyone else's name there but mine!"

"Have a bit of faith, Grace," Matt said, ladling out a bowl of porridge. "You never know—they might have decided they want you for the star part, the Swan Queen!"

Grace spluttered with laughter, and elbowed him. "It's all right for you boys, you don't have to go through this nightmare," she said.

"We wish we could!" Luke said immediately. "We boys feel a bit cheated that we don't get to even audition for a part in the show." He pretended to frown at Grace. "So think yourself lucky!"

Ellie helped herself to porridge. Luke was right, she thought. If the situation had been reversed and there were only parts for boy dancers, she wouldn't have been happy about it. "We *are* lucky to have auditioned," she agreed. "But let's hope we've all been lucky with the casting, too!"

•　　•　　•　　•

The notice board was disappointingly empty when Ellie and the others left the canteen after breakfast. "This waiting is torturous," she said with a sigh. "I can't bear it!"

"Well, it looks like the torture's almost over," Lara said, sliding her eyes sideways to where Ms. Bell, the Lower School Ballet Principal, was click-clacking her way along the corridor, a sheet of paper in her hand. "I reckon Ms. Bell is just about to put us out of our misery!"

Ms. Bell caught sight of the gaggle of eager-faced girls around the notice board and smiled. "Waiting for something, are you, ladies?" she asked, dangling the paper from her fingers. "Well, give me a bit of room so that I can pin this up, and you'll all be able to see."

Ellie stepped back obediently while Ms. Bell pinned her paper to the board. And then, as soon as the Ballet Principal had moved away, there was a surge forward, every girl desperate to read the contents . . .

Lower School Cast List for Swan Lake Little Swans
Cast A:
Natasha Merrill——Year 9
Martha Richardson——Year 9
Rachel Thulborn——Year 9
Holly Powell——Year 8
Lara McCloud——Year 8
Bryony Andrews——Year 8
Grace Tennant——Year 8 *
Ellie Brown——Year 8 *

"Yes!" Ellie yelled.

"I'm in! At last . . . I did it!" Grace said, looking dazed.

"Oh, Grace—fantastic! About time—you so deserve it," Ellie said warmly, forgetting Grace's coolness of the day before. She turned to hug her friend. "We'll be dancing together!"

But Grace was already whirling around with Bryony. "I can't believe it!" Grace was saying to Bryony. "I'm so pleased we're in the same cast!"

For a moment, Ellie felt a little lost—but then Lara came up and saw her name on the list. With a jubilant shriek she flung her arms around Ellie and began an impromptu jig. "Both of us in Cast A, Ellie—we'll be in the opening night!"

Laughing, Ellie danced with her. Around them she could hear other friends calling out, just as excited.

"Oh! There's my name—on the Cast B list!" Isabelle was squealing. "And you too, Kate—and Megan, oh, and Alice as well! We're all Cast B little swans!"

Bryony had stopped whirling with Grace by now, and was jabbing at the Cast A list. "Hey, what does this star mean, by Ellie and Grace's names?" she asked.

Ellie and Lara abandoned their waltz and came over to look, too. At the bottom of the cast list, there was another asterisk. Beside it, a line of type read:

These dancers will also perform in Act One.

Ellie felt as if she was about to faint with happiness. She was a little swan—*and* she was one of the dancing girls! Two parts! Could this get any better? "Luke! Luke!" she shouted, seeing him making his way towards her. "I got in! I'm in *Swan Lake*! I got *two* parts!"

As Luke hugged her, Ellie felt choked up with joy.

"And here you had me preparing a better-luck-next-time speech for you," he said teasingly.

"I know," said Ellie. "I'm just as surprised as you are," she said, practically floating on air. But then Ellie caught sight of Molly making her way back to the dorm alone. Molly didn't get picked, she realized, feeling a stab of pity for her friend. Poor Molly—the only girl in their dorm not to be selected.

Ellie saw that Grace and Bryony had noticed Molly slip off,

too—they were already hurrying after her. Ellie stepped out of Luke's arms. "See you later," she said to him. "I'm just going to catch up with Molly, okay?" Sisterhood was the order of the day, she thought to herself as she followed. Time to show the girls that she had room for them as well as Luke.

•   •   •   •

"I'm fine, honestly," Molly kept insisting. "Really . . . I never expected to get picked in the first place, and you three did soooo well. Plus, it's great that you're all in the same cast—you'll be dancing on The Royal Opera House stage together!" She smiled a watery smile.

Grace hugged her. "You know, it's totally because of you and Bryony that I got my parts, Molls," she said warmly. "So thank you. Your pep talk worked wonders. I owe you big time."

Molly shook her head. "You don't need to thank me," she said. "You got your parts because you're an amazing dancer, not because of anything else."

Bryony hugged Molly next. "We'd better get ready for our first lesson," she said reluctantly. "Are you sure you're okay?"

Molly nodded and started sorting out her exercise books. "I'm fine," she said. "As long as you let me have your autographs so that I can sell them on eBay when you're all prima ballerinas in a few years' time!" She grinned, suddenly looking much more her usual cheerful self. "I'll make a fortune!"

• • • •

That afternoon, as she and her friends got warmed up for ballet, Ellie could hardly wait for Ms. Black to arrive. Their teacher would surely have seen the cast lists, and wouldn't she be thrilled that so many of her students had been picked? She might even be able to give them some details about the steps they would be performing. Ellie smiled to herself as she sank into a deep *plié*. Oh, she just felt so happy!

"Good afternoon, everybody," Ms. Black said just then, coming into the studio. She was smiling, Ellie noticed, and her dark eyes looked particularly sparkly. "Well done, all of you who have been picked to be little swans. Fantastic news! I felt like cheering when I saw so many of your names on the cast lists. I'm really looking forward to seeing you all up on the stage." Her eyes crinkled as she smiled even more broadly. "Yes, I'll be coming to watch *both* casts perform," she went on, "and I'm really looking forward to it. I know you're all going to be wonderful!"

Ellie beamed at her teacher. It made it even more real, having Ms. Black talking about being in the audience, watching them.

Lara put up her hand. "Ms. Black, what's going to happen with the rehearsals?" she asked, her eyes shining. "When do they start—and will we be going to The Royal Opera House for them?"

"Rehearsals start very soon—this week, I believe," Ms. Black replied. "A rehearsal schedule will go up on the board tomorrow.

And that schedule will detail where all of the practice sessions are to be held. Sometimes the school bus will take you up to The Royal Opera House, where you'll be coached by one of The Royal Ballet's ballet masters or mistresses. I shall accompany you to some of those rehearsals, along with other Royal Ballet School teachers, so that we can see what you are working on. We shall then continue rehearsing with you here in school."

Lara winked across at Ellie, who grinned back. It all sounded sooo exciting! Ellie turned to Grace, hoping to exchange a friendly smile with her, too, but Grace was whispering something to Bryony instead.

Ms. Black clapped her hands together. "Now! It's a quarter past two already and we haven't danced a single step. Let's get started."

Ellie worked happily through her warm-up and danced through the first part of the class with a permanent smile on her face. She felt as light as air as she went through her *port de bras,* and danced as if she could spin and spin through endless *pirouettes* once they progressed to the center work.

And then a scream of agony ripped through Ellie's happy thoughts. She whirled around to see Lara lying on the floor, white-faced and clutching at her right ankle.

"Oh, help . . . it hurts!" Lara gasped, her eyes squeezed shut with pain. "It really, really hurts!"

Chapter

5

The pianist stopped playing at once, and Ms. Black rushed to Lara's side. "We need to get you to the sick bay," she said, her eyes anxious at the sight of Lara's obvious pain. She turned to Ellie. "Ellie, will you run and fetch the nurse, please? I don't want to move Lara until one of the medical staff is here."

"Sure," Ellie gulped, sprinting out of the studio at once. She couldn't help fearing that this looked a bad injury. Of course, they'd all had twists and sprains before, but the way Lara had screamed in such agony—it seemed like something worse.

And what about Swan Lake? she suddenly remembered as she raced along the corridor. *Will Lara be all right for* Swan Lake?

She panted into the nurse's office, her words tripping out of her mouth. "Ms. Black sent me—one of the students fell in the Ashton Studio—she's in a lot of pain . . ."

The nurse was with Scott Atkinson, The Royal Ballet School's doctor. They both got to their feet at once and rushed with Ellie back to the Ashton Studio.

Lara was still sprawled awkwardly on the floor, crying and

very pale. Ms. Black was crouched beside her, holding her hand. Someone had fetched Lara's sweat suit jacket and had draped it around her shoulders. The other girls looked on, all of them quiet and worried-looking.

Calmly and carefully, Dr. Atkinson felt along Lara's shin and calf. Lara winced and cried out again.

"Do you think it'll be okay?" Lara gasped, with a frightened wobble in her voice. "Do you?"

"Well, Lara, hopefully it's just a nasty twist and you'll be right as rain," Dr. Atkinson told her, "but we need to get you examined at the hospital." He turned to the nurse. "I'll take her. When we get back to sick bay, could you organize some transport for us, please, Nurse?"

"Of course," the nurse replied. She patted Lara's shoulder comfortingly.

"Okay, Lara, we're going to help you up really gently," said Dr. Atkinson. "Can you hook an arm around each of our shoulders? Good girl. That's it. Ready, Nurse?"

The nurse nodded and, slowly and carefully, they lifted Lara up from the floor.

Lara's eyes locked onto Ellie's. "Can Ellie come with me while we wait in the sick bay?" she pleaded.

Ms. Black nodded. "Of course," she said. "Ellie, put on your sweat suit so that you don't get cold." She gave Lara's hand a squeeze. "I'll check up on you later, Lara. I do hope everything's okay."

Lara's eyes welled with tears all over again. "So do I, Ms. Black," she whispered.

•   •   •   •

They slowly made their way along the corridor to the sick bay, and the doctor and nurse lowered Lara gently down onto a bed. The nurse then went off to her office to organize some transport to the hospital.

"So how did this happen, Lara?" Dr. Atkinson asked, down on the side of the bed next to her.

Through her tears, Lara managed to explain how she'd gone over on her ankle. "I felt this sort of tearing inside," she sobbed. "And then the worst pain I've ever felt in my life." She looked up at Dr. Atkinson. "What do you think it might be?" she asked, her mouth trembling.

"I think it may be what's called a high ankle sprain, Lara," the doctor replied quietly.

"What does that mean?" Lara queried, wide-eyed and fearful. "Is it really bad?"

Dr. Atkinson hesitated a moment and Ellie held her breath. "It can be serious, Lara," he answered. "It involves the ligament between the two bones in your lower leg. And I'm concerned that you may have torn or ruptured other ligaments as well . . ." He picked up a nearby phone. "But let's not assume anything. I'll phone the hospital and let them know we're on our way. We need to get an MRI scan to determine exactly the extent of your injury."

Lara let out a huge sob. "What if my leg is ruined?" she cried, tears spilling down her cheeks in misery. "What if it's all over? What if I never dance again?"

•　　　•　　　•　　　•

Ashen-faced, Ellie returned to the ballet studio. Dancing was the last thing she felt like doing now. "I promise I'll let you know as soon as we hear anything," the nurse had told her.

Ellie walked along the corridor, her mind in a whirl. Poor Lara. Was it only this morning that the two of them had been waltzing around giddily at the news that they were both going to be in *Swan Lake* together? How quickly life could change! From being one of the greatest days of Lara's life, this was no doubt fast becoming one of the worst.

It could have been me, Ellie thought, wrapping her arms around herself tightly. *It could have been any of us. Lara's a good dancer—she's not clumsy, she doesn't often make mistakes. But a slight slip . . . a twist . . . a loss of balance—and that was that.* How many times had Ellie herself misjudged a step and stumbled during ballet class? Hundreds. Thousands. Only today, Lara had really paid the price.

Ellie could hardly bear to think what must be running through Lara's head right now. It was just about the worst possible thing that could happen to a dancer—they all lived with the terrible, terrible fear of being injured and ruining their career.

Ellie pushed open the studio door, trying her best not to cry. And then, as the whole class stopped what they were doing and stared at her, willing her to give them good news, she felt the tears running down her face. "She's gone to the hospital," Ellie said in a small voice. "She needs an X-ray. The doctor thought . . . the doctor thought it could be serious."

Nobody could even think about dancing after the news of Lara's hospital visit, so Ms. Black said they would finish the class early. Ellie felt as if she was sleepwalking through a horrible dream through the rest of the afternoon. All she could think about was Lara's white, tearful face. The glory of the *Swan Lake* cast list seemed a very long time ago.

"It's her birthday in a few days as well," Ellie remembered sadly, when she and the others were back in their dorm. "I hope she's back in school by then. It'll be awful if she has to celebrate her birthday in the hospital all alone."

"We'll have to go and see her if she is still there," Molly said at once. "We could take in a cake and some presents and cards—"

Mrs. Parrish, the Year 8 housemother, popped her head around the door just then. Mrs. Parrish was usually very smiley and cheerful—but right now, she looked very serious. "Hi there, girls," she said quietly. "I've just had a call from Scott at the hospital. Lara's had the scan, and I'm afraid it's what he suspected—a syndesmosis sprain and ligament rupture."

"And that's bad?" Molly asked in a half-whisper.

Mrs. Parrish nodded. "It can be," she said. "When Lara went over on her ankle, the ligament connecting the two bones in the lower shin was totally damaged."

"So what does that mean?" Ellie asked.

"Well . . ." Mrs. Parrish said. She sounded reluctant to give an answer, Ellie thought, and she felt a horrible lurch inside.

"Will she be able to dance again?" Grace asked. It was the question that Ellie hadn't dared voice, and a hush fell over the room as they all gazed up at Mrs. Parrish's face, willing her to reply, *Yes, of course . . .*

"Hopefully, yes . . ." their housemother said eventually. "According to Mr. Atkinson, there's at least a fifty percent chance that Lara will recover enough ankle stability to continue with classical ballet."

There was a sharp intake of breath from the girls.

Bryony stifled a sob. "A fifty percent chance!" she cried.

"And how long will it be before the doctors can tell if Lara will dance again?" Ellie asked. The words came out as a whisper.

"Not for a few weeks, unfortunately," Mrs. Parrish replied. "Lara's still in a lot of pain. They're going to set her leg in plaster and keep her in the hospital overnight. Hopefully, she'll be back at school tomorrow, on crutches. Dr. Atkinson said that the plaster will come off in a fortnight or so, and she'll wear a special boot to support her foot and shin from then on. But it will be a while after that before the doctors can really see how the injury is healing."

Tears rolled down Ellie's face. "I can't believe it," she said. "I just can't believe it. Poor Lara!"

Mrs. Parrish nodded. "It's a terrible thing to happen," she said sympathetically. "But we all have to try and support Lara as best as we can through this. She's going to need all of our help—we all have to stay strong for her sake." She came over and gave Ellie a hug, then each of the others in turn. "I know you're very upset about this. We all are," she said. "But try to think about Lara. Knowing her as we do, I'm sure she won't want to see you all crying over her. She'll want you to be positive and optimistic, don't you think?"

Ellie nodded and blew her nose. Mrs. Parrish was right. They had to try to be positive for Lara's sake. But this news was sooo dreadful!

Dear Diary,

Today has been like a rollercoaster. First, the joy of finding out I had a part in Swan Lake—and then the devastation of Lara getting injured. There's no way Lara will get to be a little swan now. But worse—much worse—what if she never dances again?

It's all anyone can talk about, and all the girls have been in floods of tears all evening. Luke just hugged me and hugged me, but even that didn't make me feel much better. This is truly the saddest day I can remember at The Royal Ballet School.

The next morning at breakfast, it seemed very strange to have an empty chair at the Year 8 table. Lots of the girls had red-rimmed eyes from crying the night before, and nobody had slept very well.

"Do you think she'll be back this morning?" Grace wondered aloud, buttering some toast and taking the tiniest nibble out of it.

Ellie shrugged. "I hope so," she said. "I just want to give her a massive hug."

"Me too," Bryony echoed.

"I think all of us feel like that," Kate said quietly.

"We will have to look after her, I think," said Isabelle. "Especially on her birthday this week . . . we must do something to make her smile."

The whole morning, Ellie kept expecting Lara to hobble into one of their lessons, but she didn't. It wasn't until they'd finished lunch and had gone upstairs to get changed for ballet that they saw their friend again.

•   •   •   •

Ellie was first up to the dorms after lunch. When she opened the Billiard Room door, she was about to cross straight into the

Room Off when she heard the distinctive lilt of Lara's Irish accent and headed directly to the West End instead. There was Lara perched on the end of her bed, one leg plastered, looking pale and unhappy. Mrs. Parrish was sitting next to her.

"Hi, Lara," Ellie said. She paused, suddenly feeling awkward. She was meant to be acting supportive, right? But Lara wasn't an idiot. Ellie didn't want to patronize her by pretending everything was going to be just fine. "I'm glad you're back. How are you doing?"

Lara gave a sniff, and suddenly her face crumpled. "Not very well," she said in a muffled voice, her shoulders shaking with sobs.

Mrs. Parrish put an arm around her and passed her a handful of tissues. "All right, Lara," she said gently. "We'll get through this."

"We will," Ellie said as staunchly as she knew how, even though she herself felt like crying at Lara's words, too. She glanced up to see some of the other girls filtering into the dorm. "We're going to get through it together, Lara, you'll see. You're a strong, strong person. You've got a tough dancer's body—and you're tough inside, too. If anybody can get through this, it's you."

But Lara was shaking her head and crying still, even as Isabelle and Kate rushed over to try to console her. "But what if it's over for me?" she sobbed, crying even harder. "All my dreams, my dancing . . . what if I'm finished?"

Dear Diary,

I can still hear Lara crying from here. She's just cried on and off all afternoon and evening. She is absolutely devastated. I completely sympathize with her, but what do you say? How can you comfort somebody who feels as if they might have lost everything?

I tried my hardest to get her to come and hang out in the common room, or down in the pool room to take her mind off what's happened, but she didn't want to do anything. After a while, I went to find Luke to cheer me up but I couldn't shake the image of Lara's haunted face out of my head.

We were talking about it tonight, Luke and I, saying what a wake-up call it was to all of us. Our bodies are really so fragile—all it takes is one bad twist or fall to ruin everything. I can't imagine what Lara must be going through right now. If I thought I was seriously in danger of never being able to dance again, I'd be absolutely heartbroken. I can't even bear to think about it.

The next morning, Lara was still white-faced but had been able to stop crying. Ellie watched her friend hobble her way through the canteen on her crutches. Lara's face was usually so animated, with her sparkling green eyes and her mouth that was almost always twisted into a grin. Today she looked dazed, her face blank of all expression, as if she was hardly there.

Ellie ladled out some oatmeal porridge for herself and then noticed that Lara had stopped by the pile of trays. "Are you okay?" Ellie asked, going over with her bowl in hand.

Lara's mouth trembled as if she were about to cry again. "Actually, can you help me carry my tray?" she asked.

"Of course!" Ellie said, feeling bad that she hadn't figured it out for herself.

Ellie helped Lara get her breakfast, and then they both went to sit down. There was a rather subdued feeling among the Year 8s. It was as if nobody felt they could be happy right now, Ellie thought. To be smiling and joking as normal would somehow have seemed disrespectful to Lara, when she was in the middle of such a painful time.

Before anyone had eaten very much, Mrs. Parrish appeared in the canteen and came over to where Molly was sitting at the table. "Molly, when you've finished your breakfast, Ms. Bell would like to see you in her office," she said in a low voice.

Molly gulped. Ms. Bell was the Lower School Ballet Principal. "Why?" she asked, sounding apprehensive. "Have I done something wrong?"

"I think she wants to speak to you in private about something," Mrs. Parrish said, "but I don't think you've done anything wrong, no."

Molly put her toast down and pushed back her chair. "Suddenly, I don't feel like eating that," she said. "See you all later, guys—I hope!"

Ellie raised her eyebrows at Luke. "Strange," she commented. "I wonder what's going on?"

"It can't be anything like bad news about her family," Grace said thoughtfully. "Ms. Bell wouldn't see her about anything like that. It must be something to do with ballet."

Ellie noticed that Lara flinched at the word "ballet" and decided to change the subject fast. "Has anyone heard from Sophie lately?" she asked quickly, referring to their friend who'd been at The Royal Ballet School the previous year, but was now at a drama school. *Totally obvious change of subject, Ellie*, she thought to herself—but hey, anything to save Lara's feelings.

Molly came back after a few minutes and sat down at the table.

"What was all that about?" Bryony asked her.

"All what?" Molly asked. She busied herself buttering her toast all over again, not looking anyone in the eye. Her cheeks were very pink, Ellie noticed, and her eyes were really bright. Whatever was going on?

"Come on, spill the beans," Grace urged. "What did Ms. Bell want to talk to you about?"

"Oh, not much," Molly said, shifting rather uncomfortably in her chair. Again, she talked to the table, rather than answering Grace directly. "Actually, I think I'll leave the rest of this toast—it's stone cold. See you all back in the dorm." Without another word, she pushed her chair back and left the canteen.

"That was weird," Ellie commented, watching her go. It wasn't like honest, straightforward Molly to be secretive. And Ellie was sure there was something she wasn't telling them. But what?

•　　•　　•　　•

Up in the dorm after breakfast, Ellie, Bryony, and Grace all walked in to see Molly on her cell phone, talking excitedly. "I know!" she was squealing. "Isn't it just the—" Then, at the sound of the door being opened, she swung around and stopped mid-sentence. "Anyway, I'd better go," she said, blushing furiously. "I'll phone you later for a proper chat. Okay. Love you, bye!"

She clicked off the phone and stood there, looking the picture of guilt. Then she bit her lip and ran over to close the door. "Okay, I know what you're all going to ask me," she said in a low voice. "And I'll tell you three—but you must promise me you won't tell anyone else. Not yet."

"What? What is it?" Ellie asked, unable to stop the words bursting out of her. "We promise, Molls. Not a word."

"The secret stays in this dorm," Grace added solemnly.

Molly had a strange expression on her face. She'd looked elated when she'd been on the phone, and there was a flicker of that same elation left in her eyes, mixed with something else. A guilty, feeling-bad kind of look.

Molly looked at the floor. "Well, I don't quite know how to say this," she said. "I sure as anything don't know how I should feel about it. But I'll just come out with it, and tell you—I'm going to be in *Swan Lake* after all."

"Wow!" Ellie said, hugging her friend. "That's amazing!"

Molly looked unhappy at the praise. "Well, it's kind of amazing," she said awkwardly. "And kind of not. You see . . . it's Lara's part. That's the only reason I'm in. Because Lara's out."

A weighty silence fell. Molly sighed. "Exactly," she said. She wrung her hands, looking agitated. "It feels a bit funny, like sneaking in through the back door when everyone else has gone through the front. And how can I be really happy about it, when by rights, Lara should be dancing in that cast, not me?"

Ellie hugged her friend. She understood Molly's split reaction. It was great to have gotten a part, of course—but the fact that she got it because of Lara's injury wasn't so great. "Lara will understand," she said. "And she'll be pleased that *you* got the part, rather than someone she didn't know. If she can't dance it, then who better?"

"Thanks, Ellie," Molly said. "I hope she does see it that way. I didn't want to tell her at the breakfast table with everyone there. I need to pick my moment, get her on one side and tell her before anyone else finds out and gets to her first—that's why I made you promise to keep mum."

"Of course we will," Grace said at once. "And try not to feel bad. You obviously did really well at the audition—you earned the part. And I'm sure Lara will be pleased for you, too."

"She will," Bryony added, hugging Molly. "Well done, Molly. I'm really pleased we're all going to be dancing together. Once Lara knows and gives you her blessing, which I'm certain she will, then you won't feel so awkward about it, I bet."

Ellie nodded. "Maybe you can speak to Lara alone during break time," she suggested. "The sooner the better, I guess."

Molly nodded. "That's the other thing," she said. "I need to tell her this morning, at some point—because our first rehearsal is this afternoon!"

After Molly's announcement, Ellie could hardly concentrate for the rest of the morning. What a crazy week this was turning out to be!

During physics, never the most interesting lesson in Ellie's eyes anyway, she turned her head to see what Luke was doing. He and Matt were sitting just to the right of her and Grace. He was scribbling something on a scrap of paper and looked up, seeming to feel Ellie's gaze upon him. Then he folded the paper into a tiny airplane and aimed it at Ellie with a grin.

Ellie grinned back as it landed in front of her. She picked it up and unfolded it to read:

U R v quiet 2day, what's up? Found out Molly's secret yet?

Ellie felt her cheeks turn red at Luke's second question. Well, she *had* found out Molly's secret, but she'd agreed not to say anything until Molly had had a chance to speak to Lara, hadn't she? But then again . . . Luke *was* her boyfriend. And you weren't supposed to have any secrets from your boyfriend, were you? That's what all the magazines said. And even though she knew she shouldn't, she just couldn't resist letting him in on such an exciting bit of gossip . . .

TOP SECRET—don't tell anyone, not even Matt, she scrawled hastily, *but Molls has been asked to dance in Swan Lake instead of Lara!*

Then she folded it up into an airplane again—well, she tried to, but hers wasn't quite as neat as Luke's—and when Mr. Lewis, their physics teacher, was writing something up on the blackboard, she threw it across to Luke.

"Luke Bailey! What was that I just saw flying onto your desk?" came Mr. Lewis's voice almost immediately.

Ellie jumped. Had Mr. Lewis grown eyes in the back of his head all of a sudden? He must have turned around from the board the very second she'd thrown the note.

"Nothing, sir," Luke said innocently, as he leaned an arm across the airplane.

Mr. Lewis put down his piece of chalk and came over to stop in front of Luke's desk. He held his hand out. "Note, please," he demanded.

"What note, sir?" Luke replied, still trying to get away with it.

Ellie held her breath.

Mr. Lewis's eyebrows came together in a frown. "The note under your arm, Luke Bailey," he said crossly. "I saw you put it there. Give it to me, please."

Ellie felt a sinking feeling in the pit of her stomach. Oh, no. She really didn't want Mr. Lewis to see the note. Any sneaky note was bad enough, but this one, with the top-secret information about Molly written on it, was really not meant for anybody else's eyes!

Luke, clearly realizing there was no getting away with this one, handed the scrap of paper over to Mr. Lewis.

Please, please don't read it, Mr. Lewis, Ellie shouted inwardly. *Please—I'll do my physics prep early for the rest of the year, anything—just throw that piece of paper in the bin—right now!*

Mr. Lewis turned to Ellie. "And this note came from you?" he asked.

"Yes, sir," she confessed.

"Well, then," Mr. Lewis said, unfolding the paper casually, "let's see what is so urgent that Ms. Brown simply can't wait until the end of my lesson to tell Mr. Bailey."

"Mr. Lewis—that's a private message!" Ellie said in alarm. She was really, *really* wishing she hadn't just written down Molly's secret. Why had she done such a dumb thing? She'd promised she wouldn't breathe a word to anyone!

Mr. Lewis raised his eyebrows as if he didn't care. Then he began to read aloud. "You are very quiet today, what's up? Found out Molly's secret yet?"

There was a gasp from Molly and she spun around in Ellie's direction, her eyes wide and shocked.

Grace was staring at Ellie in horror, too. "You didn't," she mouthed. "You didn't tell him, did you?"

Ellie squeezed her eyes shut for a moment, willing the classroom to disappear. But unfortunately, she had no such luck. "Please don't read the rest out loud, sir," she pleaded, feeling as if she were about to be sick. This was like a bad dream. Caught out by her teacher—Molly and Grace both glaring daggers at her—Lara about to find out the secret that Molly wanted to break to her in private . . .

"Intriguing!" Mr. Lewis said sarcastically. "Molly's secret, eh?

I can see why you two found this so much more interesting than physics. Let's read on, shall we?"

This time Molly tried. "Please don't read out any more, sir," she said, shooting a panicked stare at Ellie. "It really is a private message."

But Mr. Lewis went on reading. "Top secret. Don't tell anyone, not even Matt, but Molls has—" He broke off, and glanced over at Lara. Then, with a sharp look at Ellie and Luke, he crumpled up the note and put it in his pocket. "Ellie and Luke, I hope that will be a lesson to you," he said sternly. "I won't tolerate passing notes in the classroom—it's rude and very distracting. Is that clear?"

"Yes, sir," Ellie mumbled. She hardly dared look at Molly or Grace. She was desperately relieved that Mr. Turner hadn't finished reading her note, but felt utterly mortified that the whole class now knew she'd been gossiping about her friends to Luke. Worst of all had been the look Molly had given her. An *I-can't-believe-you've-betrayed-me* look. Ellie felt her cheeks flood with color all over again at the memory. *What kind of a friend am I, to go around breaking my promises and blabbing secrets?* she thought miserably. *I don't blame Molly for looking so mad at me. I totally let her down.*

Ellie was relieved when the lesson came to an end. She glumly gathered together her books and then turned to speak to Molly. She had some apologizing to do, big time. "I'll see you later," she muttered to Luke. "I'd better go do some damage control, I think."

"Good luck," he said, squeezing her arm as she went by.

Molly was already halfway out of the classroom, flanked by Bryony and Grace. Ellie hurried up to the three of them, her face scarlet with guilt. "Molly—I'm so sorry," she said. "I was only going to tell Luke, no one else. But I shouldn't even have done that. I'm really sorry."

Molly's eyes were blazing with anger. "How *could* you, Ellie?" she accused. "After you promised you wouldn't tell anyone!"

"And I am soooo sorry," Ellie said, wringing her hands. "But—"

"But nothing," Grace snapped. "You *promised* not to say anything, Ellie! We *all* promised!"

"Imagine how Lara would have felt if she'd found out about Molly like that!" Bryony said heatedly.

"If I'd found out *what* about Molly?" came Lara's voice.

"What is going on?" Isabelle put in. "It's starting to feel as if there are a lot of secrets going around."

Molly sighed. "Lara—this really isn't the time or place," she said, holding her hands up. "Could we go somewhere in private?"

Lara looked down at her crutches rather helplessly. "Can't you tell me here?" she asked. "It takes me so long to get anywhere on these, I'll never be able to get to our next lesson if we make a detour. What is it? What's this thing I'm not supposed to find out? Is it something really awful?"

Ellie had another wrench of guilt inside her. Just what Molly hadn't wanted to happen—for Lara to find out like this!

Kate put a protective arm around Lara. "Look—if you don't

tell her, she's only going to start imagining the worst," she said.

"I'm already imagining the worst," Lara said bluntly.

Molly bit her lip. "Okay," she said. "I really didn't want to have to tell you this, right in the middle of the science corridor, but I don't have much of a choice now." She shot an angry look at Ellie, who flinched. Then Molly went on. "Lara, the reason Ms. Bell wanted to see me this morning is because she wants me to take over for you in *Swan Lake*."

There was a moment's silence, and Lara nodded. Then she reached across and hugged Molly awkwardly with one arm, still leaning on a crutch. "Well done, you," she said in a muffled voice. "Well done, Molly. Good for you. That's brilliant."

Molly hugged her back. "Are you sure? Are you sure you don't mind?"

Lara shook her head, but her eyes glistened with tears. "You'll be a brilliant swan," she said warmly. "You must be so excited."

"I am," Molly replied, looking as if she might cry, too. "Thanks for being so nice about it. I was dreading telling you. I didn't want to rub salt in the wound, you know, I thought . . ."

Lara shook her head again. "I knew I wouldn't be able to dance the part as soon as I went over on the floor like that," she said. Her voice was shaking, Ellie noticed. "I've got my head around that already. I'm glad it's you who got it, Molly. Promise."

"Thanks, Lara," Molly said, sounding relieved. "But hey—we're going to be late for computer studies if we don't get a move on."

Molly and Lara went off the corridor together, followed by

Kate and Isabelle.

"Lara took it really well," Ellie said to Bryony.

Bryony shot her a hard look. "That's because *Lara* is loyal to her friends."

"I guess we know where *your* loyalties lie these days, Ellie," Grace finished. "And it's clear that it's not with your *girlfriends* anymore."

And, without another word, the three of them stalked off together, leaving Ellie staring after them, feeling completely awful.

She slowly followed them down the corridor, where, to her great relief, she saw Luke was waiting further along. "Are you okay?" he asked. "I heard the tail-end of that. It sounded as if Grace was pretty mad at you."

"She was, and Molly was. They all were," Ellie said miserably. "Not that I blame them. I shouldn't have told you."

Luke slipped an arm through Ellie's. "Hey, no harm done. I didn't even get to read what you wrote, anyway, before Mr. Lewis nabbed it. Don't worry."

Ellie leaned against him gratefully. "That's a relief," she said, snuggling into him. "And I'm sorry I got us both into trouble in the first place. Honest, I swear Mr. Lewis must be psychic, the way he just seemed to *know* I'd sent you that note at that very second."

"I think it was the aerodynamics of your plane that let its flight down," Luke said teasingly. "Next time, Ell, fold it a bit more carefully and it'll fly better."

Ellie laughed. "Next time? There won't be a next time," she said. "Not in physics lessons, anyway."

•   •   •   •

For their second lesson of the morning, computer studies, Ellie usually sat with Grace, right near Molly and Bryony. But when she walked in to the classroom this time, Grace was already sitting in a threesome with Molly and Bryony—and they'd reserved no space near them. The message was quite clear: Grace didn't want to sit with Ellie anymore. Ellie felt as if she'd been slapped in the face.

"Come and sit with me and Matt instead," Luke said quickly, seeing her hurt expression.

"Thanks," Ellie said shakily. "I will. But first, I need to try and talk to the girls."

She walked over to Grace, Molly, and Bryony feeling jittery with nerves. "Guys, please," she said. "I've said I'm sorry. I really and truly am. And I've learned my lesson. I promise I won't tell a secret again." She paused, but nobody said anything. "I made a mistake, okay?" she went on. "A really dumb mistake. And Luke didn't even get to read the note before Mr. Lewis took it away."

Molly shrugged, and turned away. Bryony and Grace didn't even look at her.

Before Ellie could say anything else, Mrs. Sanderson had

walked in. "Good morning, everybody," she said. "In your seat please, Ellie. This is computer studies, not a social club!"

Ellie sat down feeling as if she'd had yet another rap on the knuckles. Thank goodness she still had the first *Swan Lake* rehearsal to look forward to that afternoon, she reminded herself. If it wasn't for that, she'd be tempted to go back to bed for the rest of the day!

•   •   •   •

The first student rehearsal for *Swan Lake* was scheduled for two thirty P.M. at The Royal Opera House. After a hurried lunch, the chosen Year 8 and 9 girls all piled into the school minibus to be taken into central London. Bryony and Molly got on the minibus first and sat together, then Grace made a point of sitting with Kate, so Ellie sat next to Isabelle. Ellie tried to act like this wasn't a big deal, but she felt hot with awkwardness. She and Grace had always partnered each other from day one at The Royal Ballet School. Now Grace was making it quite clear she wanted nothing to do with Ellie. Ellie wasn't sure how much more of her friend's anger she could bear.

Ellie's mood lifted, though, as the school minibus pulled over outside The Royal Opera House. Yes! They were really here—and she was about to take part in her very first rehearsal for *Swan Lake*. This was the stuff of dreams, all right.

The girls got changed, then were shown to one of the practice studios where a Company Ballet Master was waiting for them.

"Good afternoon, little swans," he said with a smile. "I'm Mr. Parks, and I'm going to be rehearsing with you quite a lot in the run-up to the first performances. I presume you have all done a class, so just warm your feet up and then we'll begin."

Ellie went over to the barre, feeling so excited. It was just a regular barre in a regular studio, she told herself—yet somehow, knowing that all her favorite Royal Ballet dancers would have warmed up in this very same studio made her feel all quivery. All these good feelings were almost strong enough to help her forget everything unpleasant that happened earlier in the day.

Once they were ready to start the rehearsal, Mr. Parks came and stood before them. "First of all, I'd like to say congratulations on being picked for *Swan Lake*," he said with a smile. "You are clearly all very good dancers—and have done extremely well to be here now."

Ellie felt herself smiling back at him. Praise from the Company Ballet Master felt like the best praise on earth.

"However," he went on, "although you have all been judged as being good dancers within your class setting, dancing in the *corps de ballet* is a very different matter. While you're in your usual ballet class, it doesn't matter terribly if your timing is a fraction out—but when you're onstage at The Royal Opera House, dancing in a group of people, then it does matter. And it will be noticed! In the *corps*, it is essential that you dance as one at all times. So, as swans, you need to be aware of each other constantly. Timing is absolutely crucial."

Ellie felt a little nervous at his words. She knew he was right. Being the only swan to dance out of sync with the others would guarantee that a dancer drew attention to herself for all the wrong reasons.

Mr. Parks clapped his hands. "So let's make a start by splitting you into two groups, and then we'll practice coming onstage in two lines." He quickly chose Grace, Bryony, and Molly—and then passed by Ellie and chose a Year 9 girl called Rachel Thulborn as the fourth. Seeing a relieved look flit over Grace's face, Ellie felt sick to her stomach. She wondered if Molly and Bryony were glad she had not been chosen to be in their group, as well.

Holly shot Ellie a puzzled look. She'd missed the whole Molly/ Lara drama earlier and was clearly wondering why Ellie was being left out. "What about Ellie?" she asked.

"She'll have to come with us," one of the Year 9 girls, Natasha, said.

"Sure," Ellie tried to hold her head high as she joined the other group. *It's not important,* she told herself firmly as Mr. Parks came over and began arranging Grace's group in height order. *It's not such a big deal.* Yet she could feel her cheeks turning hot, and she couldn't bring herself to look over at Grace and the others. *They don't like me anymore,* a voice said in her head, and she pressed her lips together hard. All of a sudden, she felt horribly close to crying.

Mr. Parks came over to arrange Ellie's group, then returned to the center of the studio. "Your coming-on steps are as follows," he said. "Step, *temps levé*, step, *pas de chat*, step, *temps levé*, step, *pas de chat* . . . and so on. As I said before, it all has to be done with precision timing. So, for each cast, we'll have both lines coming in from the side and then making two central lines around where I am now. Let's give it a go."

The music started and Ellie waited for Mr. Parks to count them in. "And one . . . two . . . three . . . step, *temps levé*, step, *pas de chat* . . ."

Ellie concentrated on following the exact beat of the music. "You all need to take off for the *pas de chat* at the same time," Mr. Parks reminded them. "A split-second late or early, and everyone in the audience will notice."

Step, temps levé, step, pas de chat . . .

Ellie was trying hard but she just couldn't stop thinking about the way she'd been snubbed by Grace and the others. *Is it all because of what happened with Mr. Lewis today?* she thought. *But I did say sorry! And I don't think I deserve to get the cold shoulder all day!*

"*Temps levé* in *arabesque*, sweetie," Mr. Parks reminded Ellie suddenly. "Come on—pay attention, please!"

Ellie shrank under Mr. Parks's gaze and tried again to stop thinking about Grace and the others. *Think about this instead,* she ordered herself. *You're not doing yourself any favors, Ell!*

"And . . . five, six, seven, eight!" came the Ballet Master's voice near her just moments later. Both lines were now in the center of the studio in their finishing positions. "Ellie—is it Ellie? You seem to be in another world. Your take-off on the *pas de chat* was off-beat almost every time. Please can we have you right here in the studio, with the rest of the students?"

"Yes, sorry," Ellie muttered. She tried to smile but really she felt like crying. This day was going from bad to worse. Any minute now, she was in danger of getting kicked out of *Swan Lake* if she didn't buck up her act!

She glanced around the room, hoping to see a supportive smile from one of her friends—anything to make her feel better!—but instead caught sight of Grace rolling her eyes at Molly and Bryony. Molly shook her head a fraction in a disapproving kind of way, and Bryony was frowning.

Hey! thought Ellie, smarting at Grace's expression. *That is so unfair! It's not like I usually get called out in ballet class for not concentrating!*

She squared her shoulders and listened to the next set of instructions as if her life depended on it. Let Grace pull faces behind her back. She'd show her—and the rest of them. She'd show them all that she could dance well enough for The Royal Opera House. *Just watch me go!* Ellie thought with determination. *Watch me go, Grace!*

At the end of the rehearsal, Ellie felt exhilarated by the precise coaching they'd just had, but dismayed, too, that she hadn't been able to dance her best for the Company Ballet Master.

The students were just about to leave when Elissa Burns, one of the Ballet Principals, stepped into the room. "Hi there," she said, smiling warmly. She was absolutely beautiful, Ellie thought, with her long elegant limbs and natural grace. "I hope you don't mind, but I was peeping through the window at you all, and just wanted to say how hard I thought you were all working," Elissa said. "Well done, all of you! I can tell already you're all going to be wonderful little swans."

"Th-thank you," stuttered Molly, who was nearest to her. "Wow. Thank you."

Ellie felt as if she could hardly move, she felt so awed to be standing near the great dancer herself. She was smiling, though. All her mixed emotions during the rehearsal were forgotten as she gazed upon Elissa as if she were in a dream.

"Well, I'll let you get back to school," Elissa said. "Nice to see you—and I look forward to rehearsing with you soon."

"Thank you. We are looking forward to it, too," Isabelle said reverently, her eyes sparkling.

Ellie felt dazed as she left the studio, the hurt feelings of earlier temporarily soothed. Wow! Elissa Burns had come to talk to them! She could hardly wait to tell Luke!

Dear Diary,
    My head is all over the place at the moment—what with Luke, Swan Lake, Lara's injury—and now Grace and the other girls being off with me. I thought this term was

going to be a dream come true, but some parts of it feel like a nightmare.

I'm going to get out of the dorm and see Luke to cheer myself up. I just don't feel like doing any prep. I especially don't want to be in the dorm while Grace is being so unfriendly. Molly and Bryony aren't talking much to me, either, but Grace is definitely the coldest. I'm really starting to get the feeling that she's jealous of Luke, and she's using what happened earlier as an excuse to get at me. It's horrible! I just wish everything would go back to normal.

Chapter

7

"Good morning, everybody!" said Mr. Best, their math teacher, as he came into the classroom the following day. "I hope everyone's got their prep ready to hand in? Great. Could you all pass your workbooks forward to me, please? Thank you."

Prep ready to hand in? Uh-oh. Ellie had a strange feeling of *déjà vu* at Mr. Best's words. She hadn't done her math prep! It had been English that she'd forgotten last week and now, somehow, she hadn't done a single equation from the list that Mr. Best had assigned them. Last night, she'd been so anxious to get out of the dorm that she'd forgotten all about doing her prep.

She turned to Luke—she was sitting with him and Matt once more, as Grace's threesome with Bryony and Molly seemed to be turning into a permanent arrangement now. "Have you done yours?" she whispered, but he was looking just as blank as her.

"Nope," he replied. "Matt, have you?"

Matt opened his prep book to show them neat rows of equations. "Read 'em and weep, kids," he said, shutting the book with a snap. He passed it forward and grinned. "You two are turning into a right pair of slackers," he said. "Too much lurving and not enough learning, eh?"

Luke elbowed him jokily. "All right, all right, *Grandad*," he said to Matt, rolling his eyes at Ellie. "Since when did you get so sensible, anyway?"

But Ellie couldn't smile about it. She was feeling too sick inside about forgetting another load of prep. Schoolwork seemed to be passing her by this term, without her being able to get a grip on any of it. *What's happening to me?* she thought miserably, as Mr. Best stacked up the prep books in a neat pile on his desk. *I used to be such a good student—and now I seem to be verging on total airhead . . .*

Luke was saying something to her but she could hardly hear him, her mind was in such a whirl. *Luke is what happened to me,* she thought. *He's such a big thing in my life, it's like something has had to give to make room for him. Is it impossible to have a boyfriend and still be able to get everything else done?*

"Thank you," Mr. Best said. "Is that everyone's?"

Ellie heaved a sigh and raised her hand. "I'm sorry, I haven't quite finished mine yet, Mr. Best," she said. It wasn't exactly the truth—she hadn't even started—but this way, at least her teacher might believe that she still cared about her schoolwork. "Is it okay if I hand mine in tomorrow instead?"

Mr. Best's smile vanished from his face. "Very well," he said. "Anybody else not handed in their prep?"

Luke put his hand up now. "Sorry, sir," he said. "I haven't

finished mine, either. I'll get it to you first thing tomorrow."

Mr. Best looked from Ellie to Luke with a thoughtful expression on his face. "See that you do," was all he said. Then he picked up his chalk and went over to the board. "Now—trigonometry. A subject very dear to my heart," he said, resuming his usual jolly tone. "Let me show you how it works."

Ellie worked diligently all lesson, making a real effort to understand the tangles of trigonometry that Mr. Best was explaining. "I guess this means we shouldn't meet up later," she said to Luke, once she'd worked through a series of problems Mr. Best had set them. "Not with last night's prep to do—and whatever's assigned today, too."

Luke shrugged. "We could meet up in the library," he suggested. "Then we could do our work together and still get to hang out a bit, too. Kind of like a study date."

Ellie wasn't convinced by the idea. She wasn't sure she'd be able to get any work done with Luke sitting next to her—they'd just end up chatting and playing around again, wouldn't they? "I'm not sure," she said doubtfully. She knew darn well she'd be able to work much better if she was alone.

"Come on," Luke wheedled. "It'll be much more fun than working in our dorms, won't it?"

At the word "dorm," Ellie's gaze flicked over to where Grace, Molly, and Bryony were whispering together at their desks. And suddenly she knew that she'd much rather be working with Luke than in the dorm, with the girls. "Okay," she said weakly. "But we've got to really knuckle down and do this prep, right?"

Luke grinned. "Of course!" he said.

Ellie smiled but wondered if she'd already made a mistake in agreeing. If only there were more hours in the day!

•　　　•　　　•　　　•

That evening, Ellie met Luke in the library, with a pile of prep and a new-found iron will to get on top of her work. "Math, and then history," she said in a determined voice as they found seats together.

"Absolutely," Luke said, opening the first page of his math prep book. "And please don't try distracting me as usual, Ellie Brown. Tonight it simply won't work!"

Ellie giggled—what a nerve! "Me distract you?" she said. "Like that ever happens!"

A boy from Year 9 frowned across at them. "Do you mind keeping it down?" he asked. "Some of us are actually trying to work in here."

"Sorry," Ellie said, taking the cap off her pen. But Luke was making a funny face at her and it was all she could do to hold back the giggles again. "Right—race you to get through this math first," she hissed. "Go!"

Ellie worked steadily through her math, and then, with barely a pause, she pulled out her history book to start work on a new assignment. She was doing great!

Luke was fidgeting in his seat next to her. "I need to stretch my legs," he whispered. "Fancy going for a walk?"

Ellie shook her head, determined to plough on with her work. "I guess I'll see you in the morning," she said.

"Oh come on, just for five minutes," Luke said, wriggling around in his seat. "We could have a quick game of table-tennis. Just five minutes." He stretched out an arm and began tickling her. "Ellie . . . you know you want to . . ." he teased.

Ellie squirmed and giggled on her chair. She was very ticklish. "Cut that out!" she laughed.

The Year 9 boy turned and glared at her. "I'm trying to work!" he said. "If you're going to mess about, go and do it somewhere else!"

Ellie's cheeks flamed. "Sorry," she said.

Luke grinned at her mischievously and Ellie gathered up her things. She couldn't stay in the library now, she felt far too embarrassed! "Come on, then," she said, once they were outside. "Five minutes—and then I'm going back to the dorm to do some work, okay?"

Luke took her hand and swung it as they walked along the corridor. "Okay," he said.

Kate and Matt were already playing table tennis when Luke and Ellie got there. Matt suggested a doubles match and Luke had agreed before Ellie could even say anything. She checked her watch. There was still time to make a start on her history later.

"And Miss Walker is triumphant, 21–17," Kate announced with

a laugh, a few minutes later. "Yes! Unbeaten! And her opponent is looking close to tears . . ."

"No he isn't!" Matt laughed, pretending to swipe her with his paddle. "He wasn't really trying, that's all."

"Yeah, right!" Kate snorted in amusement. "You're a terrible liar, Matt Haslum. You were desperate to win, as usual!"

"I'll ignore that blatant disregard for the truth, Miss Walker!" Matt laughed. "Right, me and Kate against Romeo and Juliet, then? Best of three!"

"But I—" Ellie said. *I only meant to be five minutes*, she wanted to say. But Luke was already tossing a coin to see who got to play first. Ellie picked up her paddle without saying another word. She'd gotten plenty of work done already, hadn't she? Maybe a bit of time out would be okay tonight.

•   •   •   •

The ping-pong went on for at least half an hour, with Kate and Matt claiming victory, two games to one. Ellie said good night to the boys, then went upstairs to the dorm with Kate.

She found Grace, Bryony, and Molly all in the Room Off, wrapping little gifts for Lara. *Oh, help*, Ellie thought. Lara's birthday was tomorrow—and she hadn't even gotten her a card!

"Got your math done?" Grace said, rather pointedly, Ellie couldn't help feeling.

"Yes," Ellie replied. "I guess I'd better make Lara a card

quickly. I forgot it was tomorrow."

"You can write your name in mine, if you want," Bryony offered. "I haven't sealed it up yet."

"Oh, can I? Thanks," Ellie said in relief. Thank goodness Bryony had said something friendly to her at last. "I guess I'll have to buy her a present over the weekend."

Grace raised her eyebrows. "I guess you'll have to," was all she said.

Dear Diary,
   Well, I got lots of prep done tonight, at least—but feel awful that I forgot to get Lara anything for her birthday. What's happened to my brain these days? There's always something I'm forgetting! It's different for Luke—he gets free time to do his prep while I'm rehearsing. I'm not saying I don't want to be in Swan Lake—of course I do—but it does mean I have absolutely no time to myself anymore. I'm starting to feel like a hamster that can't get off its wheel!

A week went by. The rehearsals for *Swan Lake* were becoming longer and more frequent, and Ellie felt busier than ever, plunged into a never-ending whirl of events. Some of the rehearsals clashed with her academic lessons, which meant that she had to catch up on her schoolwork in the evenings, as well as her prep. Ellie soon found she was falling even further behind with her prep.

Then, one morning after breakfast, Mrs. Parrish came to find her and asked for a word in private.

"I've asked to talk to you because I think there's a bit of a problem, Ellie," she said, once they were sitting in her office.

"What do you mean?" Ellie asked nervously.

"I mean," Mrs. Parrish went on, her eyes serious, "that a number of teachers have come to me, concerned that you're not working as hard as you could be."

Ellie dropped her gaze to the floor, hardly able to bear seeing the disappointed look on her housemistress's face. It was much worse, somehow, than if she'd been really angry with her.

"I know that the Year 8s sometimes feel as if they can slack off a little, having got through the first year of Lower School," Mrs. Parrish went on, "but I'm afraid the reality is, you can't. If you want to carry on at The Royal Ballet School, you have to put in the hours of schoolwork as well as the hours of ballet. You're here to work at both aspects of school life, Ellie. A dancer's life doesn't last forever—and you never know when you might need your academic side. Look at Lara . . . she'll need her academic studies if it turns out she can no longer dance."

Ellie nodded. She *had* been taking school life for granted lately, she knew it. And to hear that the teachers had been discussing her like that felt awful. She never wanted anyone to think that she wasn't totally dedicated to being a Royal Ballet School student!

"Sorry," she said. Her words came out in a croak.

"Right," Mrs. Parrish said, then her tone softened. "You're a good student, Ellie. That's the other thing the teachers have said, unanimously. I know—and you know, I'm sure—that you can do better." Then, to Ellie's great relief, she smiled. "Okay, lecture over. I'd better let you get to your next lesson. Don't make me have to say all of this again though, will you?"

Ellie shook her heard vehemently. "No," she said. "I'll try harder. I promise."

"Good," Mrs. Parrish said. "Well, I'll look forward to hearing better reports from your teachers, then. But if it happens again, Ellie, I'm afraid I'll have to speak to Ms. Purvis."

Ellie nodded and then walked out of the room, feeling chastened. To have someone question her commitment to The Royal Ballet School was just awful! From now on, she was going to have to be a model student—with no more slacking!

●　　　●　　　●　　　●

"I think I'm going to catch up on some prep and then have an early night tonight," Ellie told Luke after supper that evening.

He looked at her quizzically. "Is everything okay, Ell? You look a bit . . . weird."

Ellie sighed. She hadn't planned to tell Luke about her conversation with Mrs. Parrish—she felt too ashamed—but he looked so concerned, she couldn't help herself.

"I've had a bit of a lecture," she confessed. "From Mrs. Parrish. The teachers have been saying to her that I'm not working as hard as I should be."

"Really?" Luke asked. He put his arm around her and Ellie snuggled into him.

"Really," she said. "So I guess I'm going to have to try to tear myself away from you . . ."

Luke kissed the top of her head. "And I guess I'd better let you," he said reluctantly. "Are you sure you're okay? Stay and talk a bit if it'll make you feel better."

Ellie smiled but shook her head. "No—I'd love to, but . . ."

"I know," he said. "Prep. Don't worry, Ellie. It'll all be okay."

I hope so, Ellie thought as she headed for the dorm. *I sure hope so, Luke!*

A few minutes later, Ellie lay on her bed with a pile of French verbs to learn, but it was hard going. She couldn't help thinking about the awful conversation with Mrs. Parrish over and over again.

"Hello, stranger," Grace said, coming into the room just then. "Not meeting up with loverboy tonight, then?"

Ellie shook her head. "No," she said. There was something in Grace's tone that seemed a little antagonistic. Ellie rolled over on her bed. She was too tired to argue with Grace. She didn't even want to talk about Luke at all with her. Like Grace would understand anything about having a boyfriend, anyway!

"What's up?" Grace went on. "Am I not good enough to speak to now?"

Ellie rolled back over. "What do you mean?" she asked. Grace was *definitely* feeling argumentative, coming out with a question like that. And a very unfair question it was, too!

"What do I mean?" Grace echoed. "I mean that ever since Luke came along, you've had no time for me and the other girls. It's like, we never have a conversation anymore. You broke the promise you made to Molly, you forgot Lara's birthday—and you're so wrapped up in your precious boyfriend that you're doing badly in your schoolwork, too! I mean—"

Ellie interrupted, her temper rising. How dare Grace say all of this? "What's it matter to you, how I do in my schoolwork?" she snapped, glaring at Grace.

"Ellie, it matters to me because we're supposed to be friends!" Grace burst out. She shook her head. "And I feel as if I've lost you . . ." she added quietly. "You seem miles away from me these days."

Ellie sat up on her bed, instantly on the defensive. "Well, you've been horrible to me lately—you've been acting so jealous of Luke, and—"

"Jealous?" Grace repeated. "I'm not jealous. I'm sick of feeling like a spare part whenever Luke's around, that's all!"

"Well—" Ellie began, and then stopped. Grace was red in the face and looked as if she was about to cry.

"It's just . . ." Grace blurted out, interrupting Ellie. She sat down heavily on her bed, looking miserable. "That's not how you treat a friend. You've made me feel like I'm completely . . . dispensable!"

Ellie felt stunned. "But you're not! Of course you're not!" She bit her lip. She hadn't realized Grace had felt so left out. And yet, when Ellie thought about it, it was obvious. She'd been spending so much time with Luke all term—time that she previously would have spent with Grace. "Sorry," she said after a moment. "You're right. I have been wrapped up in myself and with Luke. And when you were offhand with me, I thought you were jealous, because you wanted a boyfriend."

Grace shook her head. "I just wanted our friendship back," she said in a low voice. "But you didn't seem to care."

Ellie felt awful. "Oh, Grace," she said, getting to her feet and going over to her friend. "I'm so sorry. I didn't stop and think about how you were feeling. I guess friends need as much TLC as boyfriends, right?"

"Right," Grace said. "And I'm sorry, too—sorry that I picked a fight tonight. It all just kind of burst out of me."

"I'm glad it did," Ellie said. "And I promise you'll never have to say that to me again. Our friendship is important to me, too—really important. I can't believe I was so stupid to take it for granted." She hugged Grace. "I've missed you, Grace," she said, feeling like crying.

"I've missed you, too," Grace replied. "But I'm glad you're back."

Dear Diary,

I'm glad I got things straight with Grace today—I feel so much happier that we're friends again. But that makes TWO things I've been taking for granted lately—Grace and school. I feel like I must have been living in some kind of a bubble this term. What planet have I been on??

Well, it all changes here. From now on, I'm not only going to be a model student, I'm going to be a model friend, too. There—two promises I simply have to keep!

Chapter
8

Ellie began the next week filled with resolve. She would change her ways and show her friends how much she cared about them, show her teachers how hard she could work, and show The Royal Ballet masters just how much she deserved her part in *Swan Lake*. Simple as that!

"Things are going to change," she announced to Luke on Saturday morning as they waited for the minibus to arrive for the school trip to Sheen. "You wait, Luke. New, improved Ellie coming right up."

Luke put his arm around her and kissed her on the cheek. "I didn't think that was possible," he said, grinning at her. "But I can't wait to meet her."

"She's here already," Ellie grinned back.

Once in Sheen, she and Luke chose a really nice bracelet and necklace for Lara's birthday present.

Then, on Sunday morning, Ellie worked hard on her ballet practice with Luke, caught up on her prep all Sunday afternoon, and then spent Sunday night having a girly night with her friends.

So that was quality time with Luke, prep, *and* the girls ticked off her to-do list.

On Monday evening, she worked diligently all the way through the rest of her prep until there was nothing whatsoever outstanding. Another thing ticked off on her list!

On Tuesday evening, she threw herself into the *Swan Lake* rehearsal with gusto. She loved the little swan dances they'd learned. This week, the teachers were paying close attention to the way the swans all had to kneel, as if they were settling on the lake.

"The arms are important—they are your wings," Mr. Parks reminded them. "You need to use the upper back for this movement. No bending at the waist there, Molly. Good, Ellie— your eye-line is perfect."

Ellie's heart sang with pleasure, knowing that she was dancing well and trying her hardest. Another thing to tick off her list of must-dos! Hey, she was doing well this week!

"When am *I* going to see you, though?" Luke grumbled the next morning over breakfast. "Well done for being bun-head goddess, Ell, but how about an evening as girlfriend goddess tonight?"

Ellie laughed. "Well, I've got yesterday's prep to catch up on tonight," she said. "And—"

"And you might be needed in the dorm, providing tissues and chocolate if I get the thumbs-down from the doctors later," Lara said, from across the table.

Ellie shot her a sympathetic smile. "What time is your hospital appointment?" she asked.

"Ten thirty," Lara said. She looked as though she'd hardly slept a wink, Ellie thought. "And Scott has warned me about twenty times that the doctors might not be able to give any further update about how well my leg is healing, but I'm still hoping they'll be able to give me some news."

"Oh, I so hope it's good news, Lara," Ellie said fervently. "Fingers crossed."

"Even if it's bad news, at least I'll know," Lara said, buttering her toast. Her eyes were faraway for a moment. "That's the worst of it, the not knowing. If I'm never going to be able to dance again, I just want to know—then at least I can get on and deal with it. Not knowing . . . it's a killer."

"I bet," Ellie said. "Well, at least you'll get the plaster cast off today. That must be a relief."

Lara nodded. "It itches like crazy," she said.

Bryony started talking about when she'd broken her arm a couple of years ago, and Ellie turned back to Luke.

"So . . . tomorrow, then?" he was asking.

"Tomorrow—yes," Ellie agreed. "It's a date."

"We've got a rehearsal tomorrow evening," Molly reminded Ellie.

"Oh, yes," Ellie said. "Sorry, Luke—well, if Lara's okay, then maybe we could get together quickly once I've done my prep tonight, then?"

Luke looked disappointed at this suggestion. "If you're sure you've got time to spare for me," he said, then drained his orange juice. "See you later," he said, and walked out of the canteen.

There was a moment's silence, and Ellie could feel her friends' eyes on her. She watched Luke go, feeling her spirits sinking. She was trying so hard to please everyone—she really was. She just couldn't give Luke any more time than she already was, though. Couldn't he see that?

Grace put a hand on her arm. "Are you okay?" she asked.

Ellie nodded. "Just about," she said. "Trying to be, anyway."

•   •   •   •

"Lara—you're back! How did you get on?" Ellie asked, running across to meet her in the canteen.

It was lunchtime, and Ellie had spent the whole morning either worrying about Luke's bad mood or worrying about how Lara was getting on at the hospital. Now Ellie could see that Lara was sporting a protective molded boot where the plaster had been taken off—but her eyes were red-rimmed.

"Oh, no," she said, bracing herself instinctively for bad news. "What did they say?"

"What did they tell you?" Kate asked, who'd come over too.

"Is it bad?" Isabelle asked, her dark eyes sorrowful, as she put a hand on Lara's shoulder.

Lara shook her head. "Too early to tell," she said, her shoulders slumping. Tears filled her eyes. "I shouldn't have gotten my hopes up, I know—but I was so hoping they would be able to tell me that I was going to be okay."

Ellie put her arms around her as Lara began to cry. "Oh, Lara," she said sympathetically. "How horrible, having to wait like this."

"I know," Lara sniffed. "It could be another couple of weeks yet. I can't bear it. I just can't bear it!"

"It's not bad news, at least," Molly said, rubbing Lara's back comfortingly. "I mean—they say no news is good news, don't they?"

"I know," Lara said, blowing her nose. "But right now, no news feels like the end of the world." She sighed. "I'm just not very good at being patient, I guess."

•   •   •   •

The Year 8 girls all rallied around Lara that night. Ellie's plans to catch up on her prep were abandoned, as an emergency cheer-up session was the order of the evening.

Even Luke understood that this was a crisis that Ellie needed to attend to. Poor Lara seemed to be really down again.

The following day, Luke was still a little grumpy with Ellie, though. "It's been ages since we had some proper time together," he complained as they queued up to collect their tuck boxes.

Ellie shrugged helplessly. "I know, and I'm sorry," she said. "But I've got a *Swan Lake* rehearsal next, and then tonight I have to do all my prep that I didn't get done last night." She took his hand. "Sorry, Luke. But it's not forever, is it? Next term, there won't be the *Swan Lake* rehearsals and we'll have more time together."

Luke looked down at the floor. "Next term is ages away," he growled. There was a moment's silence and then he looked up, and sighed. "Sorry to be bad-tempered," he said. "I just miss you, that's all. I feel like I've hardly seen you lately. And whenever we're together, there's always loads of other people around. We hardly ever get to spend any time alone."

Ellie nodded. "You're right," she said. They were almost at the front of the queue for tea and coffee now. "Come on," she said, suddenly dragging Luke away from the line. "I can live without a drink now. How about we go for a walk instead? Just us two."

Luke smiled. "That's the best idea I've heard all day," he said, wrapping his arm around Ellie's waist. "Come on, let's go."

Ellie leaned into Luke as they walked. Some time out was definitely the order of the day, she thought happily. "Where are we going?" she asked as they went along the corridor together.

Luke laughed. "I don't really care," he said. They went past an empty studio and Luke suddenly pulled her inside. "Here will do," he said, sitting down on the floor and leaning against the wall. "Ahh, bliss. Nobody around except me and you, Ellie Brown."

Ellie sat down next to him and he put his arms around her. "That feels better," she said, listening to the steady thump of his heart. "That feels so much better!"

The minutes went by as they chatted and laughed about everything and nothing. It was only when the studio door opened and a group of Year 10 boys came in, gazed at Ellie and Luke curiously, then went over to the barre, that Ellie's gaze flicked to the clock. "Oh, help!" she said. "I've got to go. The *Swan Lake* rehearsal has already started! I'll catch you later."

Luke jumped to his feet, too. "And I'm going to be late for character class," he gulped. He grabbed her for a quick kiss. "Good luck. Run!"

Ellie raced for the door. She could not believe she was missing a rehearsal. She absolutely couldn't believe it. She wasn't even dressed for ballet, she hadn't done her hair or anything. Oh, why hadn't she paid closer attention to the time? She couldn't believe the minutes had sped by without her noticing them!

I'm going to be in such trouble for being late, Ellie thought miserably, as she raced toward the dorm to get changed. *Major trouble!* She threw on her leotard and pinned up her hair as best she could. She was scarlet in the face and panting. Great. The teacher taking the rehearsal was going to be sooo impressed with that!

She raced back along the corridor and burst into the studio. To her dismay, Ms. Bell, the Lower School Ballet Principal, was taking the rehearsal!

"Ellie—I was wondering what had happened to you," she said. She didn't look pleased at all by Ellie's late arrival.

"I'm so sorry, Ms. Bell!" Ellie began. "I was . . ." Her cheeks flamed as she racked her brains for a suitable excuse. "I was doing my prep and got so caught up in it, I lost track of time."

There was a moment's silence and Ms. Bell looked closely at her. "Doing your prep, did you say?" she echoed.

Ellie nodded, but just then noticed the way that Molly was shaking her head and making throat-slitting motions behind Ms. Bell's back. Uh-oh. What was that all about?

"That's interesting," Ms. Bell said, with iciness in her voice. "Because I was told you had gone off for a walk with your boyfriend."

Ellie hung her head and shuffled her feet. She'd been caught out. What a disaster! "That as well," she said lamely.

"Right," Ms. Bell said. The word seemed horribly drawn out, and was followed by an awful, accusatory silence. And then the Ballet Principal added, "Well, if hanging around with your boyfriend is more important to you than rehearsing for *Swan Lake*, then perhaps you should go back to him, and I'll find someone else who can be more committed."

There was a shocked silence. Ellie could hardly believe what she'd just heard. "No," she managed to say, her mouth dry. "No, *Swan Lake* is more important to me. And I'm sorry. It won't happen again."

"I should hope not, Ellie Brown!" Ms. Bell snapped. "Now hurry up, get that sweat suit off and warm up!"

"Yes, Ms. Bell, sorry, Ms. Bell," Ellie said, taking off her sweat suit and rushing over to the barre. She caught sight of her reflection in the mirror, looking flustered and red-faced, and tried to regain her composure with a few deep breaths. She should have known things were going too well—she should have known it couldn't last!

•　　　•　　　•　　　•

Once they were up in the dorm, Ellie was expecting some sympathy from her friends, but Grace in particular didn't seem to be in a sympathetic mood. "I can't believe you forgot," she said. "What's going on in your head that you could forget a rehearsal for *Swan Lake* with The Royal Ballet?" She practically shouted the last words at Ellie, and Ellie flinched.

"I lost track of time, that's all! I was having a nice time with Luke, and—"

Grace was shaking her head. "This is really important, Ellie," she said. "Really important! More important than Luke, even!"

"All right!" Ellie cried, feeling defensive. She'd been called out once already for her lateness, by Ms. Bell. She didn't need to go through all of this again with Grace! "I was only a bit late. I just forgot, all right? I'm sorry that's such a crime!" She could feel her fists clenching. "I am trying so hard to fit everything in at the moment—it was a mistake. I forgot!"

Bryony loosened her hair from her ponytail. "Well, don't tell Lara you forgot about your rehearsal," she said quietly. "Because Lara would do anything if it meant she could dance in *Swan*

Lake—anything. And here's you, fit and healthy, and you're just throwing it away. Don't you care about ballet anymore?"

Dear Diary

I feel sooo bad about being late for rehearsal now. I mean, I felt bad enough before, really cross with myself that I could have been stupid enough to have lost track of the time like that—but as soon as Bryony threw Lara's name into the conversation, it was like a slap in the face.

Another promise to myself: From now on, I will go to every single rehearsal before the performances begin. I'll be there on time, first at the barre, the most hard-working dancer in the whole cast. I owe it to The Royal Ballet School, I owe it to Lara, and most of all, I owe it to myself.

I was so shocked when Bryony asked whether I cared about ballet anymore. Because of course I do, I really do. I've just got to convince Mr. Parks and Ms. Bell of that now.

Chapter

9

The very next morning, just after breakfast, Mrs. Parrish came into the dorm. "May I have a word, Ellie?" she asked. Her expression was grave.

Ellie nodded, and her heart gave an uncomfortable thump. From Mrs. Parrish's face, she was quite sure that the "word" was going to be about last night's rehearsal. She'd hardly slept worrying about what might happen—and when she finally had gotten to sleep, she'd had the most horrible dream about being late for the opening night of *Swan Lake* where, once she'd arrived at the dressing room, Mr. Parks had told her that her swan costume had been lost—and she had to wear her bathing suit instead!

"Sure," Ellie said, swallowing hard.

Mrs. Parrish led Ellie into the Slip, a room next to the dorm, and then closed the door behind them. "Ellie, Ms. Purvis would like to see you for a chat," she said.

Ellie nodded miserably, feeling sick inside. Oh, no. Just what she'd been dreading. "What do you think she'll say?" she asked fearfully. "Do you think she'll—" She didn't dare say the words. If the headmistress told her she'd lost her part in *Swan Lake*, Ellie would be devastated.

"I don't know," Mrs. Parrish replied. "Come and find me afterwards if you want to speak to me about it, though."

Ellie nodded again, feeling as if her legs might buckle underneath her. "Thank you," she said.

"I'm doomed," she muttered to herself as she walked towards the headmistress's office a few moments later. "I am so doomed."

Ms. Purvis's assistant told her to go straight in when Ellie reached the office. Heart thumping madly, Ellie did so.

The head teacher was sitting at her desk. She looked up as Ellie entered, her eyes serious. "Ellie, have a seat," she said.

Ellie perched herself on the edge of a chair. She felt so tense she could hardly bend her body into a sitting position.

"Ellie, do you know what this is about?" Ms. Purvis asked.

Ellie bit her lip. "Is it about yesterday? The rehearsal?" she asked in a low voice. She could hardly meet Ms. Purvis's eye, she felt so awful about it.

Ms. Purvis nodded. "It's partly about last night's rehearsal, yes," she said. "But I hear from Mrs. Parrish that she's already had to speak to you about late prep and your academic work, too. It doesn't sound as if you're managing to stay on top of everything at the moment." She gave Ellie a searching look. "I'm not saying that life at The Royal Ballet School is easy—not at all," she said. "You're under pressure to succeed in two very different aspects of life—schoolwork *and* ballet. But then, the students here are mostly very ambitious, and drive themselves to do their very best—to succeed."

"And *I* want to succeed!" Ellie burst out. "I do want to do my best, Ms. Purvis, honestly! And I've tried so hard to please everybody, really I have. But . . ." Her voice trailed away. She knew what the "but" was, and didn't want to have to say it to Ms. Purvis. *But I want Luke, too, as well as the ballet.*

"I'm sure you are trying hard," Ms. Purvis said gently. "I think you're the sort of person who *does* try hard, by your very nature. But ultimately, The Royal Ballet is putting on a performance this Christmas that hundreds and hundreds of people are going to pay good money to go and watch. And, in all fairness, we can't put dancers onstage who aren't one hundred percent committed to being there. So . . ."

"No!" Ellie gulped. She knew it was rude to interrupt, but she could hardly bear to hear what she was sure Ms. Purvis was about to say. "Please don't tell me I'm being taken out of *Swan Lake*, Ms. Purvis!" She could feel tears forming at the very thought. It was just too awful for words!

Ms. Purvis looked sympathetic as Ellie battled her tears. "I'm not saying that, Ellie," she said. "But the warning is there. If you can't keep up with all of your schoolwork as well as your rehearsals, I'm afraid you will have to forego your part in the performance. I'm not saying this to be unkind," she added, as a tear rolled down Ellie's cheek. "Quite the reverse. I don't want you to burn out, if it's all too much for you."

"It's not too much for me, I swear it isn't!" Ellie gulped, dashing her tears away. "You have my word, Ms. Purvis, that I'm committed to *Swan Lake*, and The Royal Ballet School. I promise!"

Ms. Purvis put an arm around Ellie. "Come on, don't cry," she said. "You've still got your part. And I'm glad that you *are* still committed to being here. You're too good a student to throw it all away."

Ellie hung her head as she left the office. The head teacher's words were still ringing in her ears. *You're too good a student to throw it all away,* she'd said. And throwing away her ballet career was the last thing on earth that Ellie wanted.

Dear Diary,

I can't believe what Ms. Purvis just said to me. The thought of losing my part in Swan Lake is just horrible. And for another person to be questioning my dedication to The Royal Ballet School—I can't bear it. I went to see Mrs. Parrish afterward to talk about it.

She was really kind, of course—but I feel so miserable. How have I let this happen?

That's the thing, though. I do know how this has happened—and I got the impression that Mrs. Parrish knows, too. It's Luke, isn't it? It's me having a boyfriend that's messing everything else up. I can't stop crying when I think about it like that. Because Luke is so lovely and I like him sooo much . . . yet I know that there's only one way to change this situation—and that's for me to end it with him.

I can't believe I even wrote that down—it feels so horrible and wrong and heart-breaking. But if I'm honest to myself—and I have to be honest, it's too important for me to kid myself about this—then I know it's the only answer. Otherwise, how can anything get better? How can I throw myself into being a dancer when I'm goofing around with Luke the whole time?

This feels like the worst decision I've ever had to make, but I know what I have to do: I have to tell Luke that it's over.

• • • •

Ellie felt quiet and miserable all day. She told Luke that she'd felt ill first thing, which was why she'd missed geography, because she couldn't bring herself to tell him what Ms. Purvis had said. Not yet. Not when it was still so confused in her head.

Every time Luke smiled at her or made one of his funny

remarks, it was like another wrench inside her. "What's wrong?" he kept asking her.

But Ellie just shook her head. "I'll tell you later," she replied each time. She was putting it off, she knew. Putting off the horrible conversation they were going to have to have—for the sake of both of their dancing careers, she reminded herself. She was doing this not just for her, but him, too. Although, right now, it felt as if they were both going to be a whole lot *worse* off, not better.

Finally, after supper that evening, she managed to get Luke alone. "Let's go in here," she said, and dragged him into an empty practice studio.

"Oh, good," Luke said, putting his hands on her waist. "Just what I was thinking—a bit of privacy at last . . ."

Ellie stepped out of his embrace, and he looked surprised. She took a deep breath. This was so hard. She felt so awful! "Luke . . . I got called to see Ms. Purvis today after being late for rehearsal yesterday," she said. "And she said . . ." She stopped. She couldn't say that Ms. Purvis had told her to stop seeing Luke. Ms. Purvis had said no such thing—and besides, it was such a cop-out.

She started again. "What I'm trying to say—really badly—is that . . . I think we should stop seeing each other." She swallowed, hardly able to believe she'd just said the words out loud. Silence hung between them, and Luke's eyes widened in surprise. "I mean," Ellie said, rushing to fill the awful quietness, "I mean, I still feel the same way about you. I like you so much, Luke. You know I'm crazy about you."

"So why don't you want to see me anymore?" he asked. He looked as if he'd been slapped.

"Because . . . I don't think it's good for us. I want to be with you the whole time—and I keep getting in trouble for missing prep and not turning up to my *Swan Lake* rehearsal . . ."

"That was only once!" Luke put in indignantly.

"I know, but . . ." Ellie spread her hands helplessly. The problem was, she didn't want to disagree with Luke. She hated having to say all of this. "Ms. Purvis said I'm in danger of getting thrown out of *Swan Lake* if I don't get my attitude right," Ellie went on. She could feel hot tears gathering at the memory. "So . . ."

"So you're dumping me," Luke said. He was shaking his head. "I can't believe it, Ellie. I can't believe it!"

"I'm doing it for you, too," Ellie said desperately, but the words sounded hollow even to her.

"No, you're not," Luke said. His eyes glittered with hurt.

"I am," Ellie said. "I'm doing it so that my dancing career won't be spoiled—and yours won't be, either. We have to do this—split up, I mean—so that we can both focus on our dancing." There was a sob in her voice, and she tried to reach out for one of his hands, but he pulled back. "But we can still be friends, can't we?" she asked wretchedly.

"No," he said, walking away from her. "I don't want to be friends. If you don't want to go out with me anymore, then forget it!"

Ellie wasn't sure how she managed to make her way back to the dorm, she was crying so hard, but somehow her legs took her there, and she stumbled into the Room Off and collapsed onto her bed.

"Ellie! Oh, Ellie! What's the matter?"

Ellie was dimly aware of Grace's voice, and then Grace putting her arms around her, trying to comfort her.

"What is it, Ellie? What's happened?" Grace persisted.

"It's Luke," Ellie managed to sob. "We just broke up. I . . ." But her words were lost in a fresh torrent of sobbing. The misery seemed to take over her whole body so that she ached with it.

"Oh, Ell," Molly said sympathetically. "Why did he do that? What did he say?"

"It wasn't him, it was me," Ellie cried, still weeping. Her pillow was soaked through already. "And I think I just made a terrible mistake!"

Grace hugged her and let her cry it out for a few moments. Bryony went to get Ellie some tissues and a glass of water. "Tell me what happened," Grace said after a while.

Ellie felt as if she'd lost all the energy to speak but managed to get out a brief version of events. "But the look in his eyes—it was as if he hated me," she wailed. "And now I think I totally did the wrong thing."

Grace rubbed her back comfortingly. "You are such a strong

person, Ellie," she said. "That took real guts. It must have been horrible."

"It was, oh, it was," Ellie sobbed, leaning on Grace as if she were about to keel over. "I really hurt him. And I feel so awful about that."

"I'm sure," Grace replied. "And I know it must seem really sad right now. But you made your decision—and it sounds like it was the right one. He'll see that in time, I'm certain."

"And it's not like you've lost him for good," Molly put in. "You wait—you two will be friends again in no time."

Ellie wiped her eyes and said nothing. The girls sounded confident that Luke would come round to Ellie's way of thinking, but Ellie wasn't so sure. Luke had stalked away as if he hated her, truly hated her. How ever could you go back to being friends after that?

Dear Diary,

I can't stop crying. I just feel devastated, heartbroken. Oh, Luke! What have I done? I was sure I was acting for the best, but now I just don't know. How could anything be for the best when I feel so awful?

The worst thing is, it's not like we even had a fight or stopped liking each other. I still like him just as much—and it just about killed me to make the break. Now I've really hurt him, and I feel terrible. That was the very last thing I wanted to do.

The girls have all been really understanding. Talk about friends in need. They keep telling me I did the right thing and that Luke and I will patch things up and be friends in the future, but I can't see it. All I know is that I've hurt Luke, my favorite person in the whole world. I feel like I've messed everything up now!

Chapter 10

Ellie wasn't the tearful type at all, but overnight, it was as if something inside her had dissolved. As soon as she opened her eyes that morning, she just wanted to start crying. The very instant that she caught sight of Luke in the breakfast line, she had to steel herself to prevent herself running straight out of the canteen. Thank goodness she would be escaping to The Royal Opera House that morning for a *Swan Lake* rehearsal. She'd never felt more glad to pack up her ballet things and get on the school minibus.

Ballet had helped her through many difficult situations in the past. She had danced her way through all sorts of problems, finding comfort in the familiarity of the positions, the exertion of movement. *At least I still have my ballet,* Ellie thought fiercely, as she warmed up at the barre once they'd arrived at The Royal Opera House. *And if I have to lose my relationship with Luke, then I have to make it count. I have to dance like it was worth it. I have to convince myself that I made the right decision!*

•   •   •   •

In today's rehearsal, Mr. Parks wanted Ellie and Grace to rehearse the dance the two of them would do in Act One together. As well as being little swans in Act Two, Ellie and Grace were dancing in a short scene as girls who dance around their old tutor.

"You're having fun in this scene," Mr. Parks reminded them. "You're pulling him around in a circle, sometimes by his coat tails, until he spins out of control and flops into his chair. So we need you both to use mime and gesture to demonstrate how you're feeling, all right?"

Ellie nodded. Mr. Parks coached them through the steps with Alex, one of the company dancers, who was playing the tutor.

"*Posé, temps levé, chassé, passé, pas de chat . . .*" Mr. Parks called out. "Good, Ellie! And again. *Posé, temps levé . . .* have fun with it! Let's see you smiling! And *pas de chat.* Good. And again!"

It was fun to practice with Grace. Ellie felt that she knew her friend's dancing really well by now, and they worked well together. It was so much fun that Luke was temporarily blocked out of her head. It was as if she was really living out the scene of the girl; as if for a short space of time, Ellie Brown didn't exist.

"Very good, girls," Mr. Parks said at the end. "Really good work. Ellie—you picked those steps up very well." He smiled warmly. "I think this scene is coming together very nicely. I'll see you both next week."

"Thank you, Mr. Parks," Ellie said. She felt warm with the praise, and knew that the Ballet Master was genuinely pleased with her. *I gave it my all today, that's why,* she realized with a jolt. *I chose what's important to me over a boy—and I've been rewarded.*

. . . .

When Ellie and her friends got back to school, it was lunchtime. Ellie went to the canteen, and the first person she saw was Luke, standing by the drinks machine. It was like being hit by a wave of emotion all over again. His shoulders were slumped, and he wasn't smiling or joking around like he usually did.

Ellie took a deep breath. Luke had said just last night that he didn't want to be friends—but *she* still wanted that. And she hated seeing him so miserable.

She walked up to where he stood and touched his arm lightly. "Hey," she said softly. "Are you okay?"

Luke jerked at her touch, and pulled his arm away sharply. "Fine, thanks," he said brusquely. "Never better."

He left the line without even getting his drink and went to sit with Matt and his friends.

Ouch, Ellie thought, feeling tears prickling her eyes all over again. *I guess I asked for that.*

. . . .

Ellie gazed at her reflection in the mirror. She hardly recognized herself. She was wearing a dark blue velvet dress and hat. A couple of weeks had gone by since she and Luke had broken up, and now she and the other cast members were trying out their *Swan Lake* costumes for the first time. She pointed her toe and stared at herself. She could hardly believe she was going to be wearing this dress onstage in just a few days. The opening night of the show was on Thursday and today was Monday already!

Luke had barely looked in Ellie's direction over the last fortnight, much to her dismay. Her ballet was still going well, and she was getting praise in most of her rehearsals now. She was on top of all her schoolwork, too—but it wasn't much consolation when Luke didn't want to know her anymore.

I made the right decision, I know it, Ellie kept telling herself, whenever she did well on a test, or Mr. Parks told her she'd danced well. Yet then she'd see Luke still looking guarded, and hurt, and she'd doubt the break-up all over again. Luke still seemed to hate her for it.

"Weird, huh?" Grace said, cutting into Ellie's thoughts. She, too, was in a similar blue dress and hat. They would be wearing these costumes in their scene in Act One together. "I can't decide whether or not I'm looking forward to the performance . . . or whether I should just start running away, right now!"

"Be excited," Ellie told her, coming to stand a little closer to her friend. "It's going to be great. And I'm so pleased we get to dance in a scene together, aren't you?"

Grace returned the smile. "Definitely," she said.

The wardrobe mistress bustled over just then and started checking the fit on Ellie's dress. "That's fine," she said, after a few moments. "You can try on your swan costume now."

Ellie carefully peeled off her dress and hung it up. Then she took her swan costume off its hanger and stepped into it. All white, of course, it was sooo gorgeous: a long tutu with a satin bodice, and layers and layers of net that came to just below Ellie's knees, and it had the softest white feathers sewn over it to make her look like a swan. There was also a beautiful headdress, and the wardrobe mistress showed her how to position it on the top of her head without disturbing her bun.

With a final smooth down of the wrinkled net, Ellie looked at herself in the mirror. There. An excited-looking swan grinned back at her. "I can almost believe it's going to happen now," she said to herself, feeling happier than she had ever since the break-up. "I look like a real, professional ballerina!"

●   ●   ●   ●

The Friday before the end of term there was a Christmas disco in the large Margot Fonteyn Studio. Ellie didn't really feel like going. Not so very long ago, she'd been looking forward to it—a chance for her and Luke to dance together under the mistletoe! But now she could see no fun in it.

"Come on, we'll have a good girly night," Molly said encouragingly, but Ellie just couldn't stir up the enthusiasm. All she could think about was the last disco she'd been to, earlier in the term, before she and Luke had begun dating. She'd been so jittery, and spent half the evening hoping he'd ask her to dance. It seemed a very long time ago now.

This time round, she let the girls choose an outfit for her. Then Bryony fussed over her hair, pinning it up in an elegant top-knot.

"You look gorgeous," Grace assured her, but Ellie didn't feel very gorgeous inside.

"Come on," said Lara, hobbling in to see if they were ready, "if I can go to the Christmas disco—on crutches!—*you* can go, too, Ellie. If you don't want to dance, you can keep me company instead."

Ellie tried to smile across at Lara, feeling chastened. If Lara could be so cheerful about a disco, knowing she might never be able to dance at one again, then she, Ellie, could get through the evening, too. "You're on," she said. "Let's go."

•　　•　　•　　•

Once they were at the disco, Ellie sat down with Lara away from the dance floor. She couldn't help her gaze wandering around the dancers, though, wondering if Luke was already there. Would he even stay away, not wanting to be reminded of the last disco they'd been at together?

Ellie felt her mind spinning off into a daydream. What if he did turn up, though, feeling miserable and nostalgic, just like she was . . . and he saw her, and came over, and they got to talk to one another about how sad the break-up was, and how much they'd meant to each other . . . and maybe, by the end of the evening, they could be friends again, and both feel happier?

Beside her, Ellie felt Lara stiffen and turned to see what had made her friend react in that way. And there on the dance floor—oh, she could hardly believe it!—there on the dance floor was Luke . . . dancing with Alice!

"I knew it!" Ellie gasped. "I knew he always liked her!"

"They're only having a laugh," Lara said quickly. "It's not like they're slow-dancing or anything."

"I know, but . . ." Ellie couldn't drag her gaze away. She just sat and stared as Luke twirled Alice around, and Alice's hair streamed back as she was whirled about by Luke's hand.

"Oh, this is horrible. I've got to go, Lara, right now. There's no way I'm going to stay and watch that all evening!"

Ellie rushed out, desperate to get away from the spectacle of Luke and Alice on the dance floor together.

Dear Diary,
Going to the disco was a really bad decision. Ouch! It felt like Luke punishing me, the way he danced with Alice like that. He

knew that I'd felt jealous of her last term. But how can I possibly complain, when it was me who finished things with him? Lara left the disco, too, not long after me, so the two of us watched a movie together. She said Luke had only danced with Alice the one time and that I was probably imagining anything between them, but still . . .

It sooo hurt!

*　　*　　*　　*

Thursday came around quickly. It was a big day for the Year 8 girls in more ways than one. As well as it being the opening night of *Swan Lake*, it was also the date that Lara was due to return to the hospital to see her specialist.

"We're all rooting for you, Lara," Ellie said, hugging her as Mr. Atkinson came to collect Lara from the dorm that morning. "We'll probably have gone to The Royal Opera House by the time you come out, but text us, won't you, and let us know what's happening."

Lara nodded, looking sick with nerves and pale from lack of sleep. "Good luck tonight, everyone," she said. "I won't say 'break a leg,' but . . ."

Grace hugged her. "Say 'mend a leg' instead," she suggested. "That sounds much better."

Lara smiled faintly. "It does, doesn't it? Thanks, guys. See you later."

"Bye, Lara," Ellie said, smiling back at her.

"Come on—we'd better get to class," Molly said after Lara had hobbled away. "Although how we're supposed to concentrate on schoolwork when we've got our first performance tonight, I've no idea!"

The morning seemed to drag by at a snail's pace. Ellie kept trying to catch Luke's eye, but he was still steadfastly ignoring her. Matt shot her a sympathetic look as she looked over at him for what seemed like the hundredth time, and then shrugged his shoulders.

Ellie swung her face away, her cheeks burning. Matt was a good friend, but right now she didn't want sympathy or pity. She just wanted Luke to look at her and respond to her in some way. Today of all days, Ellie just felt as if she needed to dance in *Swan Lake* with Luke's blessing. *If it were Alice going onstage tonight . . .* Ellie stopped herself before she could finish that thought. It was useless to compare the relationship she and Luke had to his friendship with Alice.

Ellie desperately wanted Luke to acknowledge that Ellie made the right decision for both of them. But it didn't seem likely to happen. So she would just have to keep blocking him out of her head. She couldn't let him affect her dancing, not after everything she'd given up.

Finally she and her friends were taken to The Royal Opera House to prepare for the opening performance.

Elissa Burns popped into the girls' dressing room as they were getting ready and gave them a smile. "Good luck, guys," she said. "You're all going to be wonderful, I just know it!"

"Th-thank you," Grace stuttered, her cheeks turning pink. "I hope so!"

Bryony checked her phone once Elissa had gone. "I don't understand it," she muttered. "Why hasn't Lara texted us? What could be happening, do you think?"

Molly shook her head. "I don't know," she replied. "She must have been seen by now."

Ellie pulled her hat brim a fraction lower on her head. "I hope it's not because . . ." she started to say, then swallowed. There was only one reason she could think of as to why Lara hadn't been in touch, and she hardly wanted to say the words out loud. Surely, if Lara had been given a good report she'd have called them right away. Yet, if it was bad news, Ellie could quite imagine how Lara might not feel like telling anybody. "Well, like we said before, no news is good news, right?" she said quickly.

"Right," Grace said. She stared down at her feet. "*Posé, temps levé, chassé, passé, pas de chat . . .*" she muttered to herself, dancing through her first steps. "Oh, Ell, I can't believe we're going to be dancing onstage in just a few minutes," she said, her eyes shining. "Everything's going to work out, right?"

Ellie was leaning against the wall, stretching out her hamstrings. "Sure," she said. "I just wish . . ." An image of Luke's face had swum up into her mind again, and she struggled to block out the cool, impersonal look on it. "I just wish I could stop thinking about Luke for five minutes," she confessed. "If I'm not worrying about Lara, then my mind just switches back to him, however hard I try."

Grace pulled a sympathetic face. "You know, if it makes you feel any better, I still think you made the right move, ending it with him," she said.

Ellie gave a wan smile. "I know," she said. "It was the right thing to do, for the sake of my ballet, and his, too. It's just . . ." She shrugged. "It's just so sad. And I can't help wishing . . ."

A commotion at the far side of the dressing room stopped Ellie mid-sentence. For there, coming through the dressing room door, was Lara. She still had the protective boot around her foot, Ellie noticed at once—but she was smiling.

"Lara!" Molly squealed. "What are you doing *here*?"

"What did they say?" Bryony asked at once.

"Are you okay?" Ellie asked, hurrying over to her friend.

Lara nodded, her cheeks still pink from the cold outside. "I've only got a minute, because I've got to take my seat! Ms. Bell has been so kind, she arranged for me to watch the performance as I couldn't dance in it. But I just had to come backstage and tell you my news," she beamed. "The doctors said that the looseness around my ankle joint isn't getting better, which means that even though I'll need lots more rehab and won't be able to dance until next term, they think I'll make a full recovery . . ." Lara finished, looking dazed at the words. "They think I'm going to be all right!"

"Oh, brilliant!" Ellie and her friends all cheered, throwing their arms around Lara and hugging her tightly. "Oh, Lara—that is so wonderful. Fantastic!"

"I know, I know," Lara laughed. "I had to come and tell you guys. I just couldn't wait until after the performance—and texting wouldn't have been the same."

"Well, we'll make sure we dance our best for you, Lara. Right, girls?" beamed Molly.

"Our *very* best," Ellie said with a smile, and felt Grace squeeze her hand. "And let's hope we'll all be in the Christmas production next year—Lara included!" she added.

Everyone cheered at that.

"Flowers for Ms. Ellie Brown!" came a voice just then, and a young woman with a Royal Opera House pass around her neck appeared in the doorway with a bunch of pink roses.

"For me?" Ellie said, in surprise. "Oh, they must be from my mom. Thank you!"

"I'd better get out of here," Lara said hurriedly, as the final call for the audience to take their seats sounded out. "You go, girls!"

Ellie buried her nose in her gorgeous flowers, breathing in their perfume. She opened the envelope eagerly. Her mom was in the audience, she knew, with her step-dad, Steve, and they'd brought along Ellie's friends from home, Bethany and Phoebe, as a special treat. How sweet of her mom to send flowers, too!

She pulled out the card, and then she nearly dropped the roses in shock as she read the message.

To Ellie,

Good luck on your opening night.

Sorry I didn't say it earlier.

Love, Luke

P.S. I was wrong—I want us to be friends.

Hope you still do, too. XO

Ellie's eyes filled with sudden tears—but these were happy, relieved ones.

"Hey—no crying! You'll smudge your makeup!" said Grace, passing Ellie a tissue at once.

"These are from Luke," Ellie said, setting the card up on the side. Not only did he say he was sorry, he wanted to be friends. It was more than she'd hoped for—and she felt so, so happy.

Grace hugged her. "And about time, too!" she said, mock-severely, but she was smiling in relief.

A call came over the intercom just then. "The performance is about to begin. Curtain call for dancers in Act One!"

Ellie held her breath in excitement. This was it!

"Good luck, Ellie!"

"Go for it, Grace!"

"Enjoy yourself, Ellie!"

Ellie stopped at the doorway with Grace and beamed at her friends. "Thank you," she said, feeling fluttery with excitement. "I will."

•   •   •   •

As Ellie stood in the wings backstage, she closed her eyes for a second, listening to the orchestra and focusing on her body. She could feel the heat from the stage lights, and could smell the greasepaint she wore on her face. Goosebumps prickled all over her as she caught a glimpse of the audience, knowing that out there somewhere were her mom and Steve, Phoebe and Bethany, and Lara, too. She felt revved up, charged with energy and music, and ready to dance.

I have worked so hard for this moment, she thought fiercely, *and it cost me Luke to get here—but right now, it feels like it was worth it. There's nowhere I'd rather be in the whole world!*

Her cue came and she was on the stage with Grace. And it felt wonderful.

Dear Diary,
    I'm still on a high from dancing at The Royal Opera House again in front of so many people. It was just amazing beyond words . . . I feel goosebumps all over again just thinking of how electrifying it was to hear that thunder of applause. And it made

it all the sweeter to dance there, knowing that Luke wanted to be friends with me. I've missed him—I've SO missed him, and I'm really glad I haven't lost his friendship forever.

Molly and Grace both had a great night onstage, too—and Bryony as well. And best of all, we get to dance in the show for the next few weeks . . . heaven!!

This term has truly made me appreciate my place at The Royal Ballet School even more. I can't wait to see what's going to happen next term—and one thing's for sure: I'm never going to take my school life for granted ever again!

GLOSSARY

ROYAL BALLET METHOD: An eight-year system of training and methodology developed and utilized by The Royal Ballet School to produce dancers with clean, pure, classical technique

ADAGE: From the musical direction *adagio,* meaning slow; slow work with emphasis on sustained positions and on balance

ALLÉGRO, GRAND ALLÉGRO, PETIT ALLÉGRO: Jumps that can be performed at various speeds

ARABESQUE: One leg is extended to the back (the name is taken from the flourished, curved line used in Arabic motifs)

ATTITUDE: *Grande pose;* one leg in the air with the knee bent either to the front or back

BALANCÉ: To rock; a swinging three-step movement transferring weight from one foot to the other

BALLONNÉ: Jumping step during which the dancer stretches one leg to the front or back, landing on the other leg with the stretched leg returning to *coup-de-pied* on closing

BARRE: The horizontal wooden bar fastened to the walls of the ballet classroom or rehearsal hall that the dancer holds for support

BATTEMENT: To beat; a beating of the legs; see *grand battement, petit battement,* and *battement frappé* for variations

BATTEMENT FONDU: To melt; a movement on one leg, bending and extending both legs at the same time

BATTEMENT FRAPPÉ: To strike; a striking action of the working foot

BATTU: To beat; an adjective to describe a beat of the feet; the term is always added on to a step to describe the additional movement, for example *changement battu*

BOURRÉE: A series of running steps that can be done on *demi-pointe* but more frequently on full *pointe*

BRAS BAS: The rounding of the arms held in front of the thighs with a small space between the hands

CHASSÉ (ALSO PAS CHASSÉ): A gliding step when the leg slides out and the other leg is drawn along the floor to it

CORPS DE BALLET: The body of dancers that form a ballet company excluding the Principals and Soloists

COUP DE PIED: Around the "neck" of the foot; one pointed foot is placed at the calf—just above the ankle—of the opposite leg

COUPÉ: To cut; an intermediary step in which one foot takes the place of the other foot

CROISÉ: To cross; a diagonal position with one leg crossed in front of the other

DEMI-PLIÉ: A small bend (of the knees) in alignment over the toes, without causing the heel, or heels, of the foot to lift off the floor

DEMI-POINTE: Rising *en pointe* only halfway, onto the ball of the foot, not completely onto the toes

DEVANT: In front; a step, movement, or the placing of an arm or leg in front of the body

DEVELOPPÉ: The unfolding of the working leg; the leg is drawn to the knee and then extended from there

ECHAPPÉ: To escape; a movement that begins in 5th position and moves quickly to 2nd position either by sliding to the ball of the foot or as a jump from 5th position to 2nd position

EN CROIX: In the form of a cross; a four-step movement that begins from a closed position and takes the leg to the front, side, back, and side again

EN DEDANS: Inward; indicates the direction of the working leg (counterclockwise) or the pirouette (toward the supporting leg)

EN DEHORS: Outward; indicates the direction of the leg (clockwise) or the direction of the supporting leg during a pirouette (toward the outer leg)

ENTRECHAT: A jump from two feet, crossing the feet rapidly in the air and landing either on one (if an odd number of crossings) or two feet (if an even number)

FONDU: To melt (bending and extending of the legs at the same time with one leg supporting the body)

FOUETTÉ: To whip; a quick movement on one leg that requires the dancer to change direction and can be performed in a variety of ways

GLISSADE: To glide; a connecting step that begins and ends in *plié*

GRAND BATTEMENT: A throwing action of the fully extended leg in any direction with controlled lowering

GRAND JETÉ: A throwing action; a high jump from one foot to the other

GRAND PLIÉ: A deeper bend (of the knees) bringing the heels of the feet off the floor

JETÉ: A jump from one foot to the other

PAS DE BOURRÉE: A linking movement done as a series of three quick, small steps

PAS DE BOURREÉ PIQUÉ: *Piqué* means "to prick"; a quick step out on one leg to the half-toe or *pointe* position during *pas de bourrée*

PAS DE CHAT: Cat's step (because the movement is like a cat's leap); a jump where the legs are lifted and lowered separately, forming a diamond shape in the air

PETIT BATTEMENT: Small beat whereby a pointed foot "beats" in front and back of the calf—just above the ankle—of the opposite leg; this exercise is done with great rapidity

PETIT BATTERIE: A general term to describe a beating of the legs
PIROUETTE: Turn (used to describe a turn, whirl, or spin); "turns" are sometimes referred to as *tours*

PLIÉ: To bend (the knee or knees)

POINTE: "Going *en pointe*" is to graduate from soft ballet shoes to the more demanding pointe shoes that have a hard box at the toe in the shape of a cone onto which the tips of the toes balance

PORT DE BRAS: Carriage of the arms; specific movements of the upper torso and arms

POSÉ: Stepping onto the full or half point with a straight knee

RELEVÉ: To rise (used to describe a rise from the whole foot to *demi-pointe* or full *pointe*)

RETIRÉ: To withdraw (drawing up of the working foot to under the knee)

REVERENCE: A deep curtsy; performed at the end of class as a mark of thanks and respect

ROND DE JAMBE À TERRE: Circle of the leg on the ground; a barre exercise in which one leg moves in a semicircle on the ground

SAUTÉ: To jump off the ground with both feet

SISSONNE: A scissor-like movement where the dancer jumps from two feet to one foot, or from two feet to two feet

TEMPS LEVÉ: Raised movement; a sharp jump on one foot

TENDU: Stretched; held-out; tight (in which a leg is extended straight out to the front *devant,* back *derrière,* or side *à la seconde,* with the foot fully pointed)

TOURS EN L'AIR: Turn in the air; a movement which involves the dancer turning while at the same time jumping straight up into the air; there are many types, mostly performed by male dancers